"I'm perfectly capable of taking care of myself."

Gina had to clarify her statement. "At least I used to be, before all this."

"Independence was your middle name, huh?" Harlan asked with a hint of smile.

She kneaded the pillow as she spoke, and Harlan listened. "I always wanted to take care of myself. That's why my sister and I lost touch. I wanted to do it on my own, but now—" She stopped, feeling the tears burn behind her eyes.

He put a hand to her lips. "Don't do that to yourself. Everyone has regrets, but don't beat yourself up over them." He smiled sadly and stood to walk away, but she reached out to stop him.

"Wait. Don't leave. I want—" She stopped.

His eyes bored into hers. "What do you want, Gina?"

"I want to feel safe. I want—" She took a deep breath and said, "You."

* * *

"A real page-turner by talented new author
Kay Thomas."
—Bestselling author Carla Cassidy

25 years of INTRIGUE

Dear Harlequin Intrigue Reader,

In honor of two very special events, the Harlequin Intrigue editorial team has planned exceptional promotions to celebrate throughout 2009. To kick off the year, we're celebrating Harlequin Books' 60th Diamond Anniversary with DIAMONDS AND DADDIES, an exciting four-book miniseries featuring protective dads and their extraordinary proposals to four very lucky women. Rita Herron launches the series with *Platinum Cowboy* next month.

Later in the year Harlequin Intrigue celebrates its own 25th anniversary. To mark the event we've asked reader favorites to return with their most popular series.

- Debra Webb has created a new COLBY AGENCY trilogy. This time out, Victoria Colby-Camp will need to enlist the help of her entire staff of agents for her own family crisis.
- You can return to 43 LIGHT STREET with Rebecca York and join Caroline Burnes on another crime-solving mission with Familiar the Black Cat Detective.
- Next stop: WHITEHORSE, MONTANA with B.J. Daniels for more Big Sky mysteries with a new family. Meet the Corbetts—Shane, Jud, Dalton, Lantry and Russell.

Because we know our readers love following trace evidence, we've created the new continuity KENNER COUNTY CRIME UNIT. Whether collecting evidence or tracking down leads, lawmen and investigators have more than their jobs on the line, because the real mystery is one of the heart. Pick up *Secrets in Four Corners* by Debra Webb this month, and don't miss any one of the terrific stories to follow in this series.

And that's just a small selection of what we have planned to thank our readers.

We'd love to hear from you, and hope you enjoy all of our special promotions this year.

Happy reading, and happy anniversary, Harlequin Books!

Sincerely,

Denise Zaza
Senior Editor
Harlequin Intrigue

KAY THOMAS

BETTER THAN BULLETPROOF

HARLEQUIN®

TORONTO • NEW YORK • LONDON
AMSTERDAM • PARIS • SYDNEY • HAMBURG
STOCKHOLM • ATHENS • TOKYO • MILAN • MADRID
PRAGUE • WARSAW • BUDAPEST • AUCKLAND

For my husband and daughter—who always believed my dream was possible and gave me the time to pursue it.

And for my son—without whom I never would have started this particular journey…
to the moon and back again.

You've made me laugh and you've made me stronger.
Life is richer than I ever imagined.

ISBN-13: 978-0-373-69379-5
ISBN-10:   0-373-69379-6

BETTER THAN BULLETPROOF

Copyright © 2009 by Kay Thomas

Recycling programs for this product may not exist in your area.

Printed in U.S.A.

ABOUT THE AUTHOR

Having grown up in the heart of the Mississippi Delta, Kay Thomas considers herself a "recovering" Southern belle. She attended Vanderbilt and graduated from Mississippi State University, with a degree in educational psychology and an emphasis in English. Along the way to publication, she taught high school, worked in an advertising specialty agency and had a very brief stint in a lingerie store.

Kay met her husband in Dallas when they sat next to each other in a restaurant. Seven weeks later they were engaged. Twenty years later she claims the moral of that story is: "When in Texas look the guy over before you sit next to him, because you may be eating dinner with him the rest of your life!" Today she still lives in Dallas with her Texan, their two children and a shockingly spoiled Boston terrier named Jack.

Kay is thrilled to be writing for the Harlequin Intrigue line and would love to hear from her readers. Visit her Web site, www.kaythomas.net, or drop her a line at P.O. Box 837321 Richardson, TX 75083.

Books by Kay Thomas

HARLEQUIN INTRIGUE
1112—Better Than Bulletproof

CAST OF CHARACTERS

Gina Rodgers—A struggling advertising artist, she's just landed the account of a lifetime when her sister mysteriously disappears and leaves behind a five-year-old autistic son. When Gina goes looking for answers, she uncovers more than she bargained for.

Harlan Jeffries—An ex-military sniper seeking redemption through working with special needs children. Harlan is Adam's play therapist and Gina's unexpected ally as they become tangled in a web of government conspiracy involving a big pharma cover-up about the vaccine-autism connection.

Adam Sutton—Gina's five-year-old autistic nephew, left behind after his mother's disappearance. Adam has just started to talk thanks to breakthrough biomedical intervention and cutting-edge therapy.

Sarah Sutton—Gina's sister (and Adam's mother) just completed a research study proving the vaccine-autism connection when she mysteriously disappears.

Senator Jordan Bell—Harlan's mentor and confidant. The man to whom Gina wants to entrust Sarah's study, if they can find the documents.

Tammy Douglas—Gina's assistant at Dixon Meyers Advertising. When Gina needs a friend, Tammy offers to help. But is she really looking after Gina's best interests?

Shaun Logan—Harlan's military associate with a mysterious past. When the police are hunting Gina and Harlan, Shaun provides transportation and a safe haven. Can he be trusted?

Chapter One

What a disaster. And this was one of her good days.

Standing outside the Fox and Hound, Gina Rodgers reached into the bottom of her handbag to fish out car keys and found her snazzy new cell phone marinating in beer.

Perfect. Her boss's jealous wife had quite a way with the cold shoulder and a pitcher of beer. All completely accidental, of course.

Right. And pigs fly.

Happy hour at the North Dallas sports bar was supposed to have been a celebration. Her celebration, thanks to today's big win on the PharmaVax Pharmaceuticals account. Finally, Gina the Screwup— Nope, not *screwup.* She didn't call herself that anymore, thanks to hours of therapy. Gina the Competent had done something right at Dixon Meyers Advertising. Not only had she done something right, but she had done something incredibly right and landed the biggest account the firm had on board.

Nonetheless, she was now covered in beer and heading home early. All because Marci Meyers couldn't stand the fact that her husband had dated Gina before he'd married her. Despite today's triumph with PharmaVax, her employment at Dixon Meyers wasn't going to last. Marcie's seething hostility aside, Gina couldn't take much more of working for Clay Meyers. The man was a weasel.

Perhaps with the pharmaceutical giant's scalp under her belt, she would be a more desirable job applicant. Creative directorships in advertising were rare, but not for those who'd landed Fortune 500 accounts. She'd have to contact a headhunter. Soon.

Her hand closed around the wet phone, and a new surge of anger hit. She'd just bought the electronic wonder yesterday. It took a moment to realize her beer-soaked purchase was now ringing like mad. She wiped the wet LCD screen on her blouse before answering, but her shirt was damp too. A missed-call icon glowed brightly in the small window.

Great. She hadn't even mastered voice mail or volume control. No surprise she hadn't been able to hear the Mediterranean jingle over the racket in the bar. She flipped open the sticky phone.

"Gina Rodgers."

"Gina, this is Harlan Jeffries, a friend of your sister's. I help out with Adam. Do you know where Sarah is?" The voice was steady with a deep Southern drawl but had an urgency that Gina caught immediately. "I've been trying to reach you."

"Sarah? No, I mean, I assume she's at home in Starkville."

"She's not."

Despite the certainty of his tone, she asked, "Are you sure? I mean, you called her house? I know she gets busy sometimes…with Adam and all." Sarah's research work coupled with an autistic son made for a rather full plate.

Behind Gina, the bar's door opened and music poured out, overpowering the man's next words. She shoved the phone closer to her head. Stuffing a finger in her uncovered ear, she struggled to hear through the static-filled reception.

"I'm here at her house. Adam's with me."

"I'm sorry, what is your name again?"

"Harlan Jeffries. I help out with some of Adam's therapy." The deep voice held a hint of impatience now. "Gina, I don't think you understand. Sarah is missing. She never came home from work last night."

Gina felt the car keys slip through her fingers and drop to the pavement, along with what felt like her stomach. "That's not like Sarah." A stupid thing to say but the only comment she could manage at the moment.

There was some mistake. Sarah couldn't be missing. She was the responsible one with the perfect job and the perfect life. Well, not so much anymore. A divorce and Adam's diagnosis had combined to make Sarah's situation anything but perfect.

"Have you contacted the police?" she asked.

"Yes, but there's a twenty-four-hour waiting period for missing persons."

She and Sarah hadn't talked much lately. Not since their last visit and subsequent argument at the lake house. Despite Sarah's good intentions, Gina didn't want or need her charity anymore.

Wrapped up in her own life and clueless about how to deal with her nephew, Gina had taken the easy way out. She'd quit calling. The flash of guilt stung. She shook her head as she thought about their last phone call…two months ago.

Pretty pathetic. Still, Sarah would have let her know if something was wrong.

"Harlan, you said you're a friend of my sister's. If you know Sarah, you know she wouldn't just leave."

"I agree, but I think it's going to take more than me saying that to the police. Like maybe a family member?"

She nodded even though he couldn't see her response. His reasoning made sense. A relative should be able to put more pressure on law enforcement officials than a friend, or therapist, or whatever this guy was.

The thought of her sister missing was so unbelievable that she was having difficulty wrapping her mind around the concept. *What in the world had happened?* The quickest way to find out would mean going to Sarah's home in Mississippi herself.

If Gina stopped to think about how she was completely torpedoing her job, she might hesitate. Hesitation was not an option. Instead, she focused on how her elder sister had always been there for her. And how she'd never been there in return.

She took a deep breath. "I'll be there as soon as possible." Squeezing her eyes shut against the vision of Armageddon she'd just rained down on her career, she waited a beat, then realized her career didn't matter a damn compared with Sarah.

"Good."

"Harlan, I have a lot of questions."

"I understand. I'll answer whatever I can as soon as you get here." His voice grew fainter on the wavering connection.

"I don't know what the flight schedule will be from Dallas to Starkville." She dug around in her wet bag for a pen and came up with an indelible marker. "I'm not sure if I can get out tonight. Give me your number, and I'll call you when I have arrangements made."

He rattled off his home and cell phone numbers, and she wrote them on the inside of her wrist. There was a long pause.

"Um…is Adam okay?" she asked.

"Yeah, he's fine right now." The reception grew worse and his words were garbled, but she could still understand him. "Thanks, Gina. Your sister…needs you." A loud, final click echoed in her ear, and he was gone.

Gina closed her phone. His last words were as shocking as the reason for his call. Sarah needed her. No one had ever said that before. Gina had always been the one in need.

DARKNESS CLOSED IN around Gina as soon as the cab pulled out of Sarah's circular driveway. Frantic with worry, she gathered her bags and hurried up the rain-drenched walk. It had been more than twenty-four hours since she'd first spoken to Harlan Jeffries.

Before leaving Dallas, she'd called the Starkville Police Department to confirm his story and discovered that trying to file a missing person's report long distance was an exercise in futility. Even getting to Mississippi had been a nightmare, what with flights and rental cars sold out because of an SEC basketball tournament. But she'd finally made it.

Tall trees lined Sarah's drive, their branches forming a canopy overhead. On the way from the airport, the cab's headlights had illuminated deep ravines on either side of Highway 82. Steep-sided embankments overflowed with succulent green kudzu. Monstrous vines wrapped around tree trunks and trailed from towering branches to give the impression of a haunted fairyland. Even from her sister's front porch, the surroundings felt spooky. And very deserted.

Why in the world was Sarah living in the boondocks? And where was she? Clammy fear crept up Gina's spine, much like the fog swirling around the cottage-style house tucked into the woods before her. She pressed her nose to the window beside the front door. The porch was cheerily lit, but inside it was dark as pitch in the foyer and beyond.

Was anyone even here?

Harlan might be asleep, or maybe he'd taken Adam to his house, since she'd told him to expect her several hours ago. She hadn't tried to call again until she was in the cab. By the time she realized her cell phone didn't get service here, on the back end of nowhere, it had been too late to do anything.

She knocked on the door, rang the bell and heard nothing but rain. After three minutes, she decided either no one was home or they slept like the dead. Despite the porch light, darkness seemed to press in around her. She was going to have to find her own way inside.

Wondering if Sarah still hid a key in plain sight, like she used to in Dallas, Gina scanned the flowerbed for the distinctive frog statue that doubled as a key safe she remembered from years past. She spotted the small stone amphibian tucked beside an Indian hawthorn bush near the sidewalk. The spare key was inside the frog's belly.

Unlocking the door, she stepped over the threshold. "Hello? Anybody home?" Her voice sounded unnaturally loud in the deep quiet. She stood there a moment, but no one answered.

Pulling her luggage across the scattered letters that had been dropped through the mail slot in the front entryway, she searched for a lamp or light switch. She groped along the wall, and her heart rate skyrocketed when she almost knocked a picture down.

Finally, she located a switch. Light from the overhead fixture illuminated the foyer and cast shadows into the surrounding rooms. She sighed a frustrated laugh at herself. Well, this certainly felt normal in an "I'm klutzy" kind of way.

After righting the crooked print, Gina scooped up the mail and stacked it along with the key on a walnut chest in the entry. She looked around, breathing in the scent that characterized every house Sarah had ever lived in.

Vanilla. Gina felt an involuntary smile tug at her lips.

Sarah loved those sweet-smelling candles and burned them year-round. For a moment Gina could believe that everything would be okay. She wanted to close her eyes and imagine this as a typical visit.

A living room was on her right, and a hallway leading to what she assumed were bedrooms was on the left. Straight ahead was the den. The dim green glow from a microwave clock indicated that the kitchen was beyond that.

Still, the house felt empty.

Turning left, she headed down the hall to make sure Harlan and Adam weren't sleeping in the back before she explored the rest of the house. She ended up in the master bedroom before discovering another light switch. With a sigh of relief, she looked up at the ceiling as she flipped the toggle. An antique lantern illuminated the room with bright slivers of light.

"Oh my God!" She heard her own words echo down the hallway.

The room was trashed. Drawers had been ripped from the cherry dresser, with the contents spread across the floor. The bed was unmade, and the mattress slashed to pieces as if someone had carved it up like a Thanksgiving turkey. One bedside table lamp was shattered, and papers littered the hardwood floor.

The bathroom was worse. The contents of the medicine cabinet had been emptied over the marble tiles. Shards of glass, various liquids and pills pooled together, looking like some mad modern art sculpture. Towels were thrown haphazardly about, and the large bathroom mirror was cracked.

Her scalp tingled with fear, but she still felt as if she were in a dream. She slowly backed out of the bathroom and moved toward the foyer, picking up speed along the way. Light from the master bedroom illuminated similar chaos in the guest room next door. She rushed toward the entry.

Rounding the corner past the final bedroom, obviously Adam's, she saw that the contents of his room were undisturbed. Light from the foyer shown on bright green walls and a cheerfully patterned rug. She stopped for a moment.

Where exactly was she running to?

A phone. I need to call 9-1-1.

Her brain stuck in slow motion as her feet glued themselves to the floor. Instead of going through her options, her faulty synapses took a lazy inventory of the room.

The only thing out of place here was a stuffed dinosaur on the floor by the desk. She gazed stupidly at the small *T. rex*, its glassy eyes catching the reflection from the hall lights. She pressed her lips firmly together and tasted the light sheen of sweat beading on her upper lip.

Think, Gina. Where are you going? Outside, with its dark and creepy atmosphere, did not seem to be a good option.

What about inside?

She strained to listen.

The house was silent.

Was she really alone?

That hadn't occurred to her. Surely whoever had done this was long gone. Still, she wanted out of the house as soon as possible.

Just call 9-1-1 and leave. She'd rather deal with the creepy atmosphere outdoors while she waited for the police. The scent of vanilla was no longer discernable. Instead, all she could smell was her own fear.

The full realization that an intruder could still be in the house thawed her frozen feet. Quickly backing out of the room, she heard a slight scraping sound behind her.

With a sickening sense of dread, she turned to identify the source of the noise. She had an impression of height and dark clothing just before the dizzying blow crashed down on her temple. She saw stars as she fell to her knees and raised her hand to ward off another hit.

Brown work boots and muddy jeans filled her vision, then there was nothing but gut-wrenching pain as everything faded to black.

Chapter Two

Voices echoed around Gina as she lay on the floor. She had no idea how long she'd been lying there, but she couldn't bring herself to open her eyes yet. This was going to be bad. Even now her head throbbed with a ferocity that left her nauseated.

The voices grew louder. One was high-pitched and excited, the other deep, calm and Southern-fried.

"Dickens here! Dickens here!" This from the child's voice.

"I know, Adam, I see him. I need you to take Mr. Dickens in the playroom."

"Watch Maddie?"

"No, no *Madagascar*. The DVD's at my house. Take Dickens in the playroom and make a picnic for us, okay?"

Picnic?

Something about this didn't make sense, but she was too incapacitated to explore that train of thought. She heard the sound of retreating footsteps and started to open her eyes. The searing pain in her skull had her quickly shutting her lids against the light. Gentle hands touched her cheek. She winced as fingertips brushed her temple.

"Can you hear me? You're gonna be okay," said a deeper, somewhat familiar voice. "I know it hurts. Just lie still. The police and EMTs are on the way."

"No." Gina's eyes flew open. She immediately squeezed them

shut again. "Don't need an ambulance. I'm hard-headed. Always have been."

There was a faint chuckle, a low, sexy sound.

Surely she wasn't hurt too badly if a voice sounded sexy at this point? Either that or she was hallucinating.

"Well, thanks for the warning, but I still think the EMTs need to look at you."

Her eyes fluttered, and the Southern drawl became paired with two craggy faces looking down at her with concern. Two faces became one as her vision cleared and a pair of light gray eyes stared at her with an intensity that would have been intimidating if she'd been more coherent.

She started to sit up and thought better of it, again closing her eyes. "Are you Harlan?" She tried peeking out of one half-closed lid.

He nodded. "You look like your sister." He held up a zippered plastic bag of ice. "Let's get this on your head. Then I want to hear what happened."

She took in a deep gulp of air when the ice touched her face and distracted herself by explaining about the extra key and letting herself inside to find the rooms ransacked. Sirens were sounding in the distance when she got to the part about being hit from behind.

Harlan continued to watch her with that unblinking stare. "The police weren't taking Sarah being missing very seriously, but I think they will now."

Gina watched him walk away to answer the door. When she saw his feet, she let out a breath she'd been holding.

White running shoes. No work boots. Thank God.

She closed her eyes once more and listened to Adam playing in another room. His voice was muffled but animated—filled with growls, cries and giggles.

Over the next half hour Gina repeated her story multiple times for the officers. The EMTs examined her and suggested she go to the hospital to get checked out, but Gina refused. Unfortunately, she knew the drill from former experience. There was nothing the doctors could do for her that she couldn't do for herself.

The young paramedic was making one last plea to get her to the hospital when Harlan spoke up. "I'm taking her to my house. Possible concussion, right?"

"What?" she asked.

"Yes," said the paramedic, speaking at the same time as Gina. "If she vomits, get her to the hospital whether she wants to go or not."

"No problem." Harlan nodded.

"Wait a minute." Gina shook her head, realizing too late that was a very bad idea and having to wait a few moments before she could focus on Harlan again. "What do you mean I'm going to your house? You couldn't possibly want to deal with me and Adam anymore. You've done more than enough."

On cue Adam squealed from the other room. Gina closed her eyes against the sound.

"I don't think you're in any shape to deal with Adam right now," he said. "You can't stay here alone, the crime-scene guys need us out, and there aren't any hotels available this weekend in town."

He had a valid point. No way could Gina handle herself and a five-year-old autistic boy for the next few hours. But Harlan's taking over irritated her. Of course, right now, with her pounding head and nausea, everything was irritating.

Adam squealed again.

Growing up, she'd always been the one needing help and Sarah had been the rescuer. Today, Gina didn't want or need help in any way, shape or form. She'd been doing a fairly decent job of taking care of herself for quite some time—up until she'd arrived in Starkville.

Damn, she hated going backward.

She took a deep breath and swallowed her irritation. "Okay, it's not like I have a lot of choice here."

"You're right." He nodded. "You don't. Let's go."

He was not making this easy, even as he took her elbow to help her to the foyer, where officers and another EMT milled about. He had the rolling suitcase in one hand, Adam's fingers clasped firmly in the other, and the stuffed *T.rex* she'd seen earlier, tucked under his arm. There was nothing left for her to do but retrieve her purse. She shoved Sarah's spare key and mail inside it for something to do with her own hands.

More flashing blue-and-red lights shone through the side windows at the front door. Another police car pulled into the drive. Dread settled in her stomach, effectively topping off the frustration she felt at not being in control. Unable to take her eyes off the two new uniformed officers dashing up the sidewalk through the rain, she knew in her gut they brought bad news. Harlan set the bag down and reached around her to open the door before they rang the bell.

"Harlan Jeffries?" asked the older of the two officers.

Harlan nodded.

"I'm Sergeant Turner. This is Detective Vasquez." He indicated the young woman beside him. His Mississippi accent was even thicker than Harlan's. "We spoke earlier today about Sarah Sutton's disappearance."

Harlan shook Turner's hand. "This is Dr. Sutton's sister, Gina Rodgers."

Turner tipped his head. "Ms. Rodgers, we've found your sister's car."

"Where?" The word stuck in her throat. Her mouth felt like cotton, and she had difficulty swallowing as a cold ball of fear settled in her throat.

"Down an embankment about five miles from here."

"Is she okay?" asked Gina. "Where is she now?" Visions of her sister hurt and stuck for hours in a kudzu-covered ditch filled her mind.

Turner exchanged an uncomfortable glance with Vasquez before answering. "Well, that's the problem. Dr. Sutton wasn't in the car."

Gina focused on breathing steadily. This felt like a bad dream that she could wake herself from if she concentrated hard enough.

"We found her purse and briefcase in the front seat, but Dr. Sutton wasn't inside. There was blood on the windshield. It looks like she could have hit her head in a crash. If that's the case, she may have been disoriented and left the vehicle. We're calling out a search team now for the immediate area."

Harlan spoke before Gina could reply. "Who's on the search team?"

Officer Turner reeled off several names. Harlan nodded as if he recognized some of them.

"We'd like to ask a few questions," Turner said. "Just about Dr. Sutton's work, her schedule and such."

"Certainly," said Gina, hoping her voice sounded more confident than she felt.

She turned and led them to the living room. Adam tagged along chattering with Mr. Dickens, his stuffed dinosaur. He was about to sit in the middle of the floor when Harlan took his arm and gently led him toward the kitchen, returning a few moments later alone.

"Adam is coloring with one of the EMTs," he said. "He doesn't realize his mother is missing yet. I didn't want him to hear us talking about it like this."

Again Gina felt that fissure of irritation at his proprietary manner, even though she knew he was right. The frustration was morphing into something dark and ugly. It wasn't his fault…but there it was. He sat beside her on the sofa, oblivious to her thoughts. The officers sat across from them.

"What does your sister do for a living?" asked the younger policewoman.

"She is a research doctor doing a study at State's vet school. I don't know a lot about the particulars, except that she is working with chimpanzees." Gina shrugged. "It sounded very exotic. Sarah loves her job. I think it gives her an escape from the pressures of having a special needs child at home."

"Can you tell me about her routine?" asked Sergeant Turner. Detective Vasquez had a small pad of paper and prepared to take notes.

Gina fought the urge to lean her aching head against the sofa back as that ugly ball of frustration mushroomed into bleak sadness. "I'm afraid I haven't been in touch with my sister lately. I can't really say."

"Oh?" said the officer, inviting an explanation.

"I live in Dallas. My sister and I haven't talked much in the past few weeks. Our lives and schedules are quite busy."

"When did you speak with her last?"

Gina felt her face turn red. "We spoke on the phone about eight weeks ago."

"Ah," Turner simply nodded.

The younger officer looked up from her note taking. "Well, since you and your sister are estranged, perhaps Mr. Jeffries can help us."

"We aren't estranged." *At least I don't think so.* For some reason it felt very important to explain the situation. "We are simply in different places in life. We used to be quite close."

Three pairs of eyes focused on her flaming face.

"It's complicated. Sarah and I are half sisters. Our mother died when we were quite young, so Sarah practically raised me.

"Two years ago Sarah divorced her husband. A couple of months later, Adam was diagnosed with autism, and she dove into researching his condition. Her father died right after that. Since then she has been extremely busy, and her life is so different. There wasn't that much holding us together anymore. We quit talking as often, and we've drifted apart."

Saying it out loud made Gina feel like more of a jerk than she had before, even though she'd left out some rather significant points.

"Perhaps Mr. Jeffries could give us some idea of her daily routine," repeated Turner. The officers looked at Harlan expectantly, totally ignoring Gina for the time being. "We need to know what her days look like, what time she goes to work, who she spends time with outside of work, et cetera."

Harlan leaned back into the sofa cushion. "I help with Adam

twice a week—Mondays and Thursdays. I know Sarah goes to the university more often than that. There are two more students who work with him on other days." He gestured toward the kitchen.

"There's a spiral notebook by the phone with all our notes. The contact info for everyone who works with him is in there. Sarah has him scheduled for fifteen to eighteen hours of play therapy a week."

Vasquez headed for the kitchen and the notebook. "Sounds expensive," said Turner. "How did you end up working for Dr. Sutton?"

Gina had been wondering the same thing. Harlan Jeffries didn't look like the typical babysitter. She'd initially thought he was a big guy, but sitting next to him, she realized he was huge. At least six foot four and well over two hundred pounds. He wore khaki cargo shorts and a black T-shirt that stretched over an impressive chest. The man obviously spent some serious time in the gym.

Possibly mid-thirties, he had shaggy dark hair shot through with gray. A five-o'clock shadow and a fishhook scar above his left eyebrow made him look dangerous and intimidating. Not Hells Angels dangerous but not at all like someone you'd hire to play with your child, either.

"A friend told me about Sarah and Adam, and that Dr. Sutton was looking for people to work with her son. She'd teach you the techniques, and you went from there."

Vasquez nodded. "What was your personal relationship with Dr. Sutton?"

There was a beat of silence before Harlan answered. "You mean, was I sleeping with her?"

His bluntness had the two officers raising their eyebrows. Despite her best efforts to focus on the carpet, Gina couldn't tear her eyes away from Harlan's face.

"Well, yes, that would be part of what we're asking," said Vasquez. She cleared her throat, obviously taken aback by his candor.

"I understand you have to ask the question," said Harlan, turning his disconcerting stare on the female officer, then Turner before resting his gaze on Gina. His voice was steady with no indication of nervousness or anger. "The answer is *no*. Sarah is totally focused on her son, and our relationship is all about Adam. We had a beer once after a particularly rough floortime session when I first started working with the boy. Beyond that, I'm not involved with her on any level but a professional one."

Turner asked more questions about daily routine, Sarah's work and friends. Harlan didn't have much to add, but that didn't stop the police from questioning him for half an hour. Despite the tension, Gina's eyelids drooped. She crossed her legs in an effort to stay alert and pushed the EMT's warnings about head injuries to a far corner of her mind.

"Okay," said Turner. "That'll be all we need for now. Where can we reach you if we need more information?"

"I'm taking Ms. Rodgers and Adam to my house." Harlan reeled off the address and phone number. The detective wrote it all down in her little book.

Gina tried to sit up straight on the sofa. He was taking over again. Damn it, she could do this herself.

"Where can we call for updates on the search?" She was surprised when her words sounded sleepy and slurred even to her own ears.

The officer handed Harlan a card. Apparently he, too thought she was too incapacitated to handle things. Gina's temper didn't even rise above a slow burn as her head continued to ache unmercifully.

Without protest she followed Harlan and Adam to a dark-colored Jeep in the drive. Every squeal and comment from her nephew felt as if it would crush her skull. She realized she hadn't even greeted the child yet or given him a hug. That was always awkward, since she didn't know exactly how to deal with him. Harlan was loading her luggage while Adam happily prattled about Dickens when it hit her like a double shot of espresso.

Adam was speaking. Real words. Real sentences.

When she'd seen him at the lake house at Thanksgiving, her nephew had mostly screeched and grunted. He'd had hardly any language at all, maybe two or three words. Now, less than six months later, he was using three- and four-word sentences. Some words were unintelligible but most she could understand.

What had changed? How had it happened? Questions swam in her head as she climbed into the vehicle and Harlan buckled Adam in behind the driver's side. The change hadn't struck her until now, and she felt a fool for not noticing earlier; but she'd been unconscious, and then everything had happened at once.

Harlan settled into the driver's seat and started the engine before she asked, "When did Adam begin talking?"

"So it's noticeable?" He put the car in gear and pressed on the gas.

"Yes. I can't believe it took me so long to recognize the difference."

Adam began an animated conversation with Mr. Dickens, complete with growls, roars and some incomprehensible natter.

"You were distracted." He sped up as they turned onto the highway.

She huffed a laugh. "That's putting it mildly." Her worries over Sarah were temporarily pushed aside in her astonishment over Adam's progress. "What's made the difference?"

"I'm not sure. Sarah's admitted she doesn't even know for certain. It's hard for me to gauge how much progress he's made, since I've only been working with him a few weeks. He was already stringing words together when I got here."

Adam squealed again rather loudly, or maybe it was just the enclosed space. Gina winced visibly and swiveled around to look at him. She couldn't see him very well in the darkness, but he was bouncing around despite being strapped in, looking like a typical five-year-old boy full of energy and fun.

Harlan turned to him and spoke quietly. "Hey, buddy, inside voice, remember, even in the car."

Adam nodded.

"Hi," Gina murmured.

Her nephew didn't reply, didn't even look up from his stuffed dinosaur. She turned back to face the road. Had she really expected him to talk to her? He didn't know her.

And whose fault is that? Gina smiled sadly. God, she'd really missed out here. Why had it taken a crisis to get her on board?

Harlan's voice brought her back to the present. "Your sister's been doing some biomedical therapies for him lately with various supplements. He probably takes two-dozen different vitamins a day. Sarah wasn't sure if it was the therapy or the supplements, but she claimed he had made some dramatic progress this winter. Something's obviously working."

More growls and giggles came from the backseat followed by muffled whispering.

"It's unreal." Gina still couldn't believe the change.

"Yeah, and it's how I know Sarah didn't just bail on him."

"I never thought that," she said.

"I know you didn't, but the cops did."

"You think they still do?"

"Not since they found her car."

Gina was silent as the reality washed over her. Her sister was missing, injured, possibly dead, and no one had any idea where she was or why this was happening. And her son, who was so incredibly disabled, was miraculously speaking for the first time in Gina's experience with him.

Rain spat against the windshield. The hiss of tires on wet pavement was the background noise for Adam's prattling. Gina leaned her still-throbbing head against the seat and closed her eyes.

Sarah, where are you?

She could feel the burning behind her eyelids as tears threatened to burst through the dam she'd constructed over the past twenty-four hours and thirty-one years. She took a deep breath before stuffing the emotions down deep inside.

Big girls don't cry.

The litany from her childhood echoed through her brain.

Sometimes they do.

She scrubbed the moisture from her cheeks.

No, they don't. The sound of a palm striking flesh faded away. She bit her lip against the pain—both past and present.

"You okay?" he asked.

She sniffed and stared at the curving road before them. "No, not really."

"We'll be at my house soon. You can lay that seat back, if you want to. I'm guessing your head is hurting a little bit about now."

"Harlan, has anyone ever told you that you have a talent for understatement?"

"No, I don't get that very often." She could hear the smile in his soothing Southern voice as she found the lever to recline the seat. Adam was much quieter now.

Turning on her side, she faced Harlan in the darkness. "So what is it exactly that you do with Adam?"

"It's called floortime. That's a type of play therapy. Autism makes communicating with people difficult. Adam doesn't play like other children. The therapy is a way of keeping him engaged so that he learns interacting with others is more rewarding than staying in his own world and not speaking."

"Like picnics?" she asked, remembering what she'd heard him tell Adam before.

"Yeah, he loves playing with all kinds of plastic food. I understand he used to stim on it pretty badly."

Stimming. Gina remembered. The last time she'd seen Adam, he was obsessed with all types of plastic model food. He would line it up and group it by color but never put it on a plate and pretend to eat it or play with it like a typical child. In December she'd searched high and low for exotic fruits and vegetables to send for Christmas.

"Did you know they make plastic models of pomegranates?" she asked.

"Yeah, he's got one of— Oh, that was from you. He likes it. Can't say it."

She heard a clicking sound as he flipped the blinker.

"Your sister used floortime and Adam's obsession with plastic food to teach him how to have a pretend picnic. It was one of the first pretend things he learned to do. He now has picnics with Dickens and me all the time."

"So what do you do when you're not playing with my nephew?"

"I'm taking a couple of courses at the college." He shrugged, "I'm sort of on vacation right now."

"Are you independently wealthy or something?" she joked.

His deep chuckle soothed her. "Only in my dreams."

"So, in real life you do what?"

"I'm in between jobs." The humor in his voice disappeared.

"Who did you used to work for?" The light from the dash glowed bright enough for her to see his jawline tense at her rather pointed question. Well, he'd have to get over being irritated. She wanted answers. Starting with who was this man who had so insinuated himself into Sarah's life? Not to mention her own.

At first she didn't think he was going to tell her. But after a moment he spoke.

"The military."

"What did you do for the military?" Figuring she'd get more answers if she kept it light, she smiled and curved her fingers to form quotation marks around the last two words.

He didn't answer immediately. The temperature seemed to plummet as silence wrapped around them. Even Adam was quiet.

"You sure you want to know?" His question was clipped, completely devoid of emotion.

A new chill in the air raised hairs on the back of her neck. "Yes."

"I killed people."

Chapter Three

Smooth, Harlan, real smooth.

Gina's swift intake of breath told him what he already knew. That was a dumbass thing to say. His self-destructive tendencies were reaching new levels.

"I was a marine sniper in Iraq," he added, hoping that would be enough of an explanation.

Even in the green glow from the dashboard, he could tell that it wasn't. He couldn't see her eyes in the semidarkness, but he knew what he'd find if he could.

Fear.

He already felt it rolling off her in waves, like heat rising from baking asphalt on a hot summer day. And when the fear faded, there would be questions. Lots of them. He was going to have to do some fast talking, or Gina Rodgers would take her nephew and be gone before morning.

Wasn't that what he'd prefer anyway?

Not that it mattered what he'd prefer. He was here to do a job. He'd made a promise to someone else besides her sister. Gina's disappearing would only complicate matters.

"Don't flip out on me, okay?" He turned toward her in the bucket seat as they waited at a red light and used his calm "trust me" voice.

Harlan had been told more than once that he had an FM radio announcer's tone. A former girlfriend had declared his voice a lethal weapon and said Harlan should talk like that only when dealing with hysterical women or frightened animals. He figured this particular situation qualified, even though Gina appeared to be holding her own for the time being.

"I shouldn't have said it that way. I'm not an ax murderer. It's been a long day. Apparently, I'm more tired than I realized."

"What are you doing here?" She was almost whispering.

He raised an eyebrow. The questions had started even sooner than he'd expected.

"I'm from Artesia, near Starkville. Just back from my third tour." He peered at her through the semidarkness, trying to make eye contact, but the dim light made it impossible.

"Did Sarah know what you did…before?"

"Yes, she knew. It didn't seem to bother her."

There was a long pause. What else could he say? *Think, man, think.* Something more soothing than "I kill people."

Apparently, he was an idiot.

"Well, that makes sense." Her voice surprised him as much as her words. She sounded steadier and more confident. "I mean, it doesn't really have anything to do with Adam or what you're doing here, right?"

"Right." He looked away, no longer able to maintain even the illusion of eye contact.

Working with Adam had everything to do with what he was doing here and what he used to do. But she didn't need to know that. Not yet, anyway.

"So do you think you'll have to go back?" she asked.

Maybe he'd done too good a job of calming her down. Now she was asking questions he didn't want to even think about, much less answer. "Not as a sniper."

"Why not as a sniper?"

"Back injury."

He certainly wasn't going to elaborate on that point. He wasn't even ready to face the truth himself. He needed to steer the conversation in another direction before it headed into shark-infested waters again.

"What happened?"

Too late. He could see fins on the horizon.

"You're awfully nosey." Even though he was trying, he couldn't quite keep the irritation out of his voice.

"It's one of my worst faults. I ask inappropriate questions. I should've been a reporter."

"Cute."

"You gonna answer the question?"

"I was wounded. Hurt my back. I can't do the PT part of the job anymore." He felt her eyes on him through the darkness. She looked at him, really looked at him. His body tensed.

The physical therapy he'd had to do since Iraq made him the picture of fitness. But that was a facade, like so many other aspects of his life. He hit the blinker with more force than necessary for the turn into his neighborhood.

"You're kidding, right?" Her voice pulled him out of his private musings. "You don't look disabled, and I don't mean that as a come-on."

For the first time he was glad it was dark, since he could feel himself blushing. "Nope. I have to do physical therapy and weights pretty much full-time to keep my back strong. Otherwise, I'd be on painkillers round the clock." He wasn't living that way, no matter what.

"Having to go to the gym every day." She shook her head. "Sounds like my own version of hell." There was a lightness to her voice that hadn't been there a moment ago. She stopped talking as he turned into the driveway.

They were finally home, thank God. He turned off the ignition. "Well, there are worse things, I suppose."

"Right." She seemed to withdraw again, obviously thinking about some of the worse things that had quite likely befallen her sister.

"Here we are." He surprised himself by how much he wanted to fill the silence. And that was crazy, since he'd wanted her to stop talking moments before. "Let's get you both inside."

He turned to look over his shoulder. Adam had been unusually quiet during his Dr. Phil moment. "I thought so."

The boy was sound asleep in the backseat, his head mashed against the door, his hands curled under his cheek. Gina turned around to stare at Adam as well.

"Let me get the door open, and I'll carry him in," said Harlan. "If we're lucky, he won't wake up till morning."

He left them in the car and unlocked the house, turning on lights and clearing the way to carry Sarah's boy up to the attic guest room. When he got back to the car, he found Gina still watching Adam sleep.

"Can you carry him with your back?" she whispered.

"Yeah, as long as I lift with my knees."

He positioned himself in a squat and pulled the forty-pound child into his arms. Without speaking, Gina followed him up the porch steps. He was grateful for the quiet as he left her in the middle of his living room to take Adam to bed.

He concentrated methodically on one task at a time, just as he'd done in Iraq. The only difference was he had no idea what would be next when he got back downstairs. His mind raced as his footsteps fell quietly on the pine treads.

What in the hell was he going to do with Gina?

WHAT IN THE HELL was she going to do?

Gina's head still hurt as she looked around the living room and tried to figure out her host. His story seemed as surreal as the fact that Sarah was missing. An ex-sniper as a child's therapist? At this point it didn't seem any more far-fetched than her sister's disappearance.

His house smelled like…burnt cookies?

One glance toward the kitchen told the story. A baking sheet covered with chocolate chip chunks of charcoal rested by the porcelain sink.

Comforted by the fact that he wasn't omnipotent, she explored the living room for some insight into Harlan Jeffries. She wanted to know more about the man she and her nephew were suddenly so dependent on. Maybe looking at his house would take her mind off wondering what had happened to Sarah.

As for his former profession, she was going to pull a Scarlett O'Hara and try not to think about it for now. From a pragmatic viewpoint, she knew there was nothing she could do to change the situation tonight. She and Adam were stuck here until morning at least.

If Sarah trusted Harlan with Adam, Gina would do the same. At least until she had more options. Options that she would have to devise all by herself.

Pushing that daunting thought aside, she stood in the center of the room to survey her surroundings. Spartan furnishings and sparsely filled bookshelves offered up few clues to Harlan's personality. A copy of the latest Elmore Leonard novel and a fitness magazine rested on the coffee table. A flattened candy bar wrapper, obviously serving as a makeshift bookmark, poked out of the book. The mantel yielded more results.

Three framed photographs.

The first was of a woman with a small boy. Most likely Harlan and his mother. The next picture was of a grown-up Harlan and another man. With lean, young faces and rifles slung over their shoulders, the two warriors were dressed in desert camouflage and standing in front of a military jeep.

The final picture was larger than the others. Harlan stood beside a bride and groom. The groom was the same man from the camouflage shot. He and Harlan both wore military dress. Another man—sixtyish, distinguished, vaguely familiar—stood beside the bride. Gina studied the photo.

All the men held raised champagne glasses, toasting the bride. Harlan beamed at the couple with a smile that positively transformed him from brooding soldier to *GQ* model. This wasn't an expression Gina had seen in the flesh. Of course, there hadn't been much to smile about since she'd met the man.

She stepped back from the mantel, feeling as if she'd invaded someone's privacy. Something brushed the back of her calf, and she jumped a foot. A small cat sidled up beside her and wound around her ankles. Gina stood in the center of the room catching her breath and trying to decide if she was having a heart attack or a nervous breakdown.

Purring like a locomotive, the cat looked at her expectantly and gave one plaintive meow. Gina felt her lips curving into a genuine smile. "Well, hello, sweetie. I never would have expected to find you here."

She sank down to the leather sofa, and the gray tabby jumped into her lap, butting its head against her hand. The warm fur was silky smooth under her fingertips. The cat's motor continued to rumble.

Sitting here like this felt so normal. And wasn't that a joke. Everything was completely out of control.

Hot tears pricked the back of her lids. God, where was Sarah? Leaning her head against the cushion, she closed her eyes, desperate to get a handle on her emotions and the situation. She took several deep breaths, scrubbed the moisture away from her cheeks and bit the inside of her lip. She had to get a grip. She couldn't help her sister if she was a quivering mass of emotion.

Her purse still hung on her shoulder, and she reached inside for a tissue, only to come up instead with Sarah's mail. She sat staring dumbly at the stack of envelopes for a moment and vaguely recalled stuffing them into her bag along with the spare key as she'd left Sarah's house.

She set the mail on the sofa cushion beside her to continue the search for tissue. True to Murphy's Law, the letters slid across the slick leather and ended up in pile on the floor. As she gathered them up, the return address on one caught her eye.

Warrick and Sullivan. Attorneys-at-law.

What did Sarah need a lawyer for? The divorce was over two years ago. The big jerk had packed up, moved back to Boston and remarried last spring. He couldn't handle Adam or his diagnosis. Sarah had talked about it at Thanksgiving.

Gina felt the stinging guilt wash over her. She hadn't handled Adam's diagnosis any better herself. The sealed correspondence crinkled in her clenched fist.

But this wasn't the firm she remembered Sarah using for the divorce. She studied the envelope marked Personal and Confidential, hesitating for about three seconds before sliding her finger under the back flap and pulling out the single typed page.

Dear Dr. Sutton:

Thank you for coming to see me last week and for sharing your preliminary research. Your review of the scientific aspect of our case was enlightening.

I believe the results of your chimpanzee study will be most helpful as we prepare for our Daubert hearing next week. If you would testify at the trial, I would consider it a personal favor. Your expertise with the material would prove invaluable for our case.

Please let me know when the final documentation we discussed is ready. My assistant, Kate Brooks, will pick it up.

As you know, we expect this case to set a precedent, and I can't stress enough the importance of confidentiality. Please do not disclose the facts (or even the nature) of your research to anyone. I look forward to working together. Feel free to call me at home if you have any questions or concerns.

Best regards,
William Sullivan

Sullivan's home phone followed.

She stopped and reread the letter, trying to put it together. What kind of case was this? She hadn't a clue.

"What are you doing?"

Harlan's voice caused Gina to tense up and suppress a slight squeal. The cat lifted its head from her lap but didn't skitter away.

"God, you scared me." She took a deep breath and put a hand on the cat's back.

"What's that?" He didn't apologize. His eyes were riveted on the letter in her hand.

"I'm not sure. It's from Sarah's lawyer, I think." She handed the page over and stroked the tabby's head while Harlan reread William Sullivan's letter twice.

When he was done, he looked at her with that disconcerting intensity and a grim expression.

"What do you suppose it means?" she asked.

"No idea. But it sounds as if she was about to testify for someone. I think we should call William Sullivan and see if he'll tell us what's going on."

"You believe this has something to do with Sarah's disappearance?"

"At this point, yes. Anything and everything could possibly be related to her disappearance." He picked up the cordless phone on the end table beside her.

"How would a chimpanzee study help with a legal case?" she wondered aloud. "It doesn't make sense."

"I agree. So let's call him. We've got his home phone number right there in the letter."

Damn it, he was taking over again. She needed to focus and right now her head was so fuzzy she hardly knew her own address.

He held the phone and stared at the letter before dialing.

"Wait a minute." *Slow down.*

He stopped and glanced up at her again. "Why are you fighting this?"

"I'm not fighting it. I mean—"

He continued that unblinking gaze.

"Hell, I don't know what I mean. It sounds bitchy and ridiculous at this point, but you're taking over. I don't deal with that very well. It's making me crazy, and I'm already crazy enough."

He sighed. "You're right."

He stopped for a moment, and she felt relieved—scarcely believing that he was agreeing with her, until he spoke again. "You are being ridiculous. Your head has got to be splitting by now, and you must be exhausted. You're not in any shape to do this. Tomorrow I'm sure it will be a different story. Tonight I'm calling Sullivan. Get over it."

She saw red and bit the inside of her lip again to keep from screaming something outrageous at him while he dialed the phone. It didn't help that he was right. Her head *was* splitting.

What was wrong with her?

That was easy. She *was* losing it.

She leaned her head back against the sofa and buried her hands in the cat's fur. Being out of control scared her almost as much as Sarah's being missing. Refusing to look at Harlan when he made the phone call, she studied the ceiling fan instead, listening as he explained who he was and why he was calling.

"I'm sorry to hear that. When did it happen?" He didn't look at her as he spoke.

"I'd like to talk with you in person if possible." He paused. "No, I understand. What time does it start?" He scribbled on a pad of paper by the phone base. "Where is that? All right. I understand. I'll be there. I promise I won't keep you long."

Gina listened with growing concern to Harlan's side of the phone call. *What was going on?*

"Thank you. We'll see you in the morning." His back was to her as he finished the call. "Good night." He clicked off the phone and slowly placed it on the charger before turning around.

"Well? What did he say?" She stared at him expectantly. "Did Sullivan have any idea what might have happened?"

Harlan's face was unreadable.

"No, he didn't. William Sullivan is dead."

Chapter Four

The house seemed unnaturally quiet, but Gina heard the hum of the refrigerator as it switched on. Harlan's words hung in the air. The ceiling fan swirled lazily overhead.

"Wh-what?" she stammered.

"He was killed two days ago. Hit by a car while he jogged in his neighborhood. I was talking to his paralegal. According to her, he was the victim of a hit-and-run."

Harlan glanced back at the phone as Gina struggled to absorb the news. "It was very strange. The paralegal, Kate Brooks, she sounded…scared."

Gina's throbbing head continued to pound even as she processed the new information. "You think it wasn't an accident?"

"I don't know. The timing is odd and awfully coincidental considering what's happened with Sarah." He shook his head again. "I'm meeting Kate tomorrow after Sullivan's funeral."

"I'd like to—"

"Alone." He interrupted.

Well, that just plain pissed her off. "I'm coming with you." *And I don't care whether you like it or not.*

"Why? In all likelihood this is some wild-goose chase."

"And if I stay home while you're out on this wild-goose chase, I'll be doing what exactly? Waiting by the phone for word on my sister? I don't think so. I'm coming with you."

She was not about to sit there all by herself with Adam, wondering when and if the police were going to call and tell her Sarah was dead.

"That's ridiculous, Gina. Besides, what will we do with Adam?"

"From what I've seen of Adam tonight, he'll do just fine." She nodded her head for emphasis. A huge mistake as the pain flared up, but she kept talking.

"I'll get him some crayons and paper and we'll have a party. We're coming with you." Her voice raised on this last part, and from upstairs they heard a wail and a loud sob that quickly escalated to inconsolable weeping.

Harlan shot her a hard look. "Great. That would be the party animal. What do you propose we do now?"

She didn't have an answer, so she stood motionless under his forceful gray gaze. Powerless and guilty. A screwup once again.

There was no need to state the obvious. She didn't know Adam well enough to comfort him. Harlan said nothing. Cries came pouring down the stairwell as he hurried up the steps. Moments later Adam's sobs quieted and turned to giggles.

Gina waited at the bottom of the stairs and listened to muffled voices. There was a very earnest discussion going on up there. Fresh guilt layered on top of old at having woken Adam after what had to have been a hard day.

Footsteps sounded on the ceiling above her head before the boy appeared on the staircase. Harlan's voice followed him down. "Peanut butter and rice cakes, buddy. No movie. That was the deal. Then straight to bed."

Harlan appeared moments later. "We're having a snack, then getting back to bed. You're helping," he announced.

Chastened and nodding, Gina followed them to the kitchen. She found a plastic knife just in time to see Harlan finish spreading the peanut butter.

Once again feeling inept, she sat at the table and watched Adam devour a peanut butter–coated rice cake. He ate without drinking anything. Just watching him made her tongue stick to the roof of her mouth. She started to say something about it but stopped herself, unsure of how to proceed.

"I'll get some sheets and a blanket so you can sleep on the sofa bed." Harlan headed down the hall to a linen closet.

He appeared to be ignoring their earlier conversation, and that served as the impetus she needed. Screwup or not, she was going to that meeting with Sullivan's paralegal tomorrow, even if they had to stay up and fight all night.

When Adam was safely back in bed she took another run at the argument. "I need to be there tomorrow, Harlan. Just to hear what's going on for myself."

"I don't understand why you think you need to be there. I'll tell you everything that's said."

"Because this is my sister. Please, I've a right to hear."

He closed his eyes. "I know I'm going to regret this." He shook his head again. He was starting to look like one of those bobble-head dashboard dogs.

"Thank you." Gina smiled at him. She wasn't sure why he'd agreed, but she was grateful and more than a little surprised. He didn't strike her as one who gave in easily.

Fifteen minutes later she snuggled triumphantly under the covers on the sleeper sofa. Her head still ached but lying flat was already making the pain more bearable. Tomorrow it had to feel better. Thankful to have won the first battle, she had the distinct impression that this was only the beginning of the war where Harlan was concerned.

Thursday morning

CRAYON-COATED PAPER covered the scarred Formica tabletop of the diner. Adam feverishly drew dinosaurs, chattering about *Apatosaurus*, *Diplodocus*, and *T.rex*. After completing a masterpiece, he would meticulously place the page in front of Gina and Harlan. She made the appropriate oohing and aahing noises, but

Harlan seemed distracted as he scanned the road through the smudged plateglass window.

Gina could tell what he was thinking from the scowl on his face. She was thinking the same thing.

Where the hell was Kate Brooks? The woman was supposed to have been here an hour ago. But she was coming from a funeral, and Gina was willing to give her the benefit of the doubt.

The scent of stale coffee and bacon grease permeated the air. The roadside diner outside of Kosciusko, Mississippi, was not into heart-healthy fare. She could feel her arteries clogging from the fumes alone. The pancakes and link sausage they'd ordered after waiting the first half hour were contributing to that sensation as well.

A weary-looking waitress topped off their high-octane coffee. Gina leaned back, finally giving into a jaw-popping yawn. She needed the caffeine, intravenously if possible.

Harlan took a deep sip of the black tar brew before breaking the silence. "I don't believe she's going to show. The funeral was over three hours ago. I thought something was off last night. She seemed skittish, spooked even."

He reached for the creamer as his phone rang. "Jeffries here." His brow creased as he listened. "Yes, Sergeant Turner."

Gina sat up straight. "Sarah?" she mouthed.

He glanced up at her, shook his head and frowned. Gina gritted her teeth and stared out the window, willing herself to be patient.

A white sedan pulled into the parking lot. She watched the window and listened to his side of the conversation as a young woman with wild red hair hurried from her car to the door.

"I didn't know we weren't allowed to leave Starkville." Harlan tilted the phone between his neck and ear. "What's the problem?" His voice was low, tense. The scowl deepened. "We'll be back later this afternoon. That's the best I can give you."

Gina watched the door as the redhead scanned the restaurant and headed toward them.

"Right, well, you do that," he said into the phone. "We won't talk again without an attorney present." He slapped the phone shut. "Damn it."

"What is it?" asked Gina. "Is there any word on Sarah?"

The redhead arrived at their booth, looking over her shoulder, wiping her nose with a tissue. She appeared nervous. Her face was splotchy as if she'd been crying.

He shook his head. "I'll explain later." Harlan stood and reached out his hand to the woman. "Kate Brooks?"

The paralegal nodded and shook his fingers. "Sorry I'm late." She sniffed and glanced over her shoulder again, her eyes moving quickly around the diner before settling on Gina and shaking her hand as well. "It took longer than I expected to get away after the service."

"I'm sorry to hear about your employer," Gina offered, struck by the contrasts in the woman's appearance. She had a pierced eyebrow and carried a Coach briefcase under her arm.

Kate slid into the booth beside her without being asked. "I don't have much time. What do you want to know about the letter?"

Her abrupt manner took Gina off guard. Harlan filled the silence. "What was the letter about?"

"Our Daubert hearing next week."

"What's that?" asked Gina.

"A Daubert hearing is where the judge decides if scientific evidence is credible enough to be admissible at trial. Dr. Sutton's study, along with her testimony, was going to provide the basis of our argument in an upcoming civil suit about thimerosal."

"Thimerosal?" asked Harlan.

"It's a mercury preservative used in some vaccines. Dr. Sutton is studying mercury's effect on the developing brain of monkeys."

"Monkeys?" asked Gina.

"Primates have a similar neurological development to humans," explained Kate.

"So, what had she found out?" asked Harlan.

"That thimerosal causes severe damage in the developing

brain. Her study showed that the toxicity level of thimerosal is actually higher than that of the mercury found in fish."

"Fish?" asked Harlan. He shifted in his seat as Adam pushed another dinosaur picture in front of them. "What does that have to do with your case?"

Gina glanced down at a purple *T.rex* and smiled encouragingly at the boy before giving her full attention back to Kate's explanation.

"We need to be able to prove that thimerosal causes neurological damage in children and specifically causes autism. Finding definitive scientific evidence of mercury-induced damage has been the real sticking point up to now in mercury vaccine litigation."

Gina stared at the table, trying to absorb the implications of her sister's research. "Who was sponsoring Sarah's study?"

Kate waved away the waitress approaching their table. "A tuna-canning manufacturer who wanted to know if the mercury levels in their product are dangerous to the general public."

"I don't understand the connection," Gina shook her head.

"The part of Sarah's study we were interested in was her control groups. One control group demonstrated that the damage to a developing brain was worse with thimerosal exposure than it was with the type of mercury exposure found in fish."

"So is it true? Does thimerosal in vaccines cause autism?" Gina asked.

"There are a lot of doctors and parents out there who believe it does. Many children who are treated for mercury toxicity improve."

Kate handed a paper-filled folder to Gina. "These are lab reports on children our firm is representing." Multicolored bars and graphs covered the pages. "Tests from kids who have improved, and in some cases recovered from their autistic symptoms, after they had the mercury removed from their bodies. That recovery wouldn't be possible with a purely genetic disorder."

"What about the recent chromosomal and genetic research in the news?" asked Harlan, reaching for the papers.

"It's fascinating and well-reported research but only applies to about 1 percent of the autistic population," explained Kate.

"These results and the children's improvement would seem like proof in itself," he said, studying the pages.

Kate shook her head. "You would think so, but it takes more than circumstantial test results. The court needs official studies, and those studies are difficult if not impossible to conduct. Almost everyone vaccinates. Where would you get the control group? Who would willingly inject mercury into their child? We've been waiting years for Sarah's kind of scientific evidence. She would be a very compelling witness given her personal experience with autism."

Gina watched Adam coloring a bright orange *T.rex* and thought of her own work and their newest client, PharmaVax. "Wouldn't that kind of lawsuit devastate most pharmaceutical companies and vaccine programs?"

Kate smiled grimly. "It'll make the tobacco lawsuits look like Judge Judy's court. The damages we are discussing are practically incalculable." She checked her watch. "Look, like I said before, I really don't have much time—"

"Please," interrupted Harlan, smiling that *GQ* grin Gina had seen only in the picture on his mantel. "We just need a little more information."

Kate stopped in the act of picking up papers from the table. Gina was sure she'd been stunned by the smile.

"I'll try and give you the short version." Kate closed her briefcase and leaned back in the booth. "For years we've been told to vaccinate our children as the government has added to the number of required shots. There are hundreds of new vaccines in the pipeline just waiting to be tested and approved. It's a multi-billion-dollar industry."

Gina watched Adam hold up another masterpiece. He smiled but wouldn't meet her eyes. "Good job," she murmured, turning to stare out the window.

A battered pickup pulled into one of the spaces close to the road. She watched a man in overalls get out and walk to the back of the vehicle, rummaging around in the bed of the truck. Dread, anger and frustration combined to make her stomach cramp and her head ache—a leftover from last night's misadventure.

If what Kate was saying was true, the implications for Sarah were frightening. Pharmaceutical companies might do anything to keep Sarah's study from coming to light. But the rational side of Gina's brain said the paralegal was being paranoid.

Kate's voice brought her back to the table. "Autism affects one out of every one hundred sixty-six children. That's basically an entire generation. Once the thimerosal autism connection is established in court, there will be an avalanche of cases to come forward. The manufacturers would do anything to keep this information from coming to light." She started to pack up her briefcase.

"Anything?" asked Harlan. He pierced Kate with that gaze Gina found so disconcerting.

The paralegal stared back before looking over at the parking lot herself once again. She frowned, and at first Gina didn't think she was going to answer. When she finally spoke, her voice was low.

"Because of her son's issues, Sarah realized the huge ramifications of her study. Once William heard about the control-group numbers, he asked if she would hold off on sending her final report to the tuna company until after our Daubert hearing. It was only a matter of delaying a few days because she was still compiling all the data from the other parts of the study."

"Did Sarah agree to wait?" asked Gina.

Kate nodded. "I thought she did. Your sister had only been finished with the initial research a couple of days when she and William spoke last week. But weird things started happening after they talked." Kate lowered her voice another notch. "Someone broke into the office, but nothing was taken."

Harlan looked skeptical.

Kate ignored him and focused on Gina.

"Since nothing was missing, we assumed it was a random burglary. Then—" She stopped and shot another furtive glance around the diner before continuing. "William told me he thought the phones were being tapped."

"What?" Harlan glanced at Gina, no longer making an effort to hide his skepticism.

Kate nodded. "I know how it sounds. Paranoid, unbalanced. I don't know that I believed him until the day before he died." She stared down at her clasped hands on the table and squeezed her eyes closed for a moment. "I was wrong not to. We were... William was followed. I saw the man, too."

"Why didn't you call the police?" asked Harlan, obviously not convinced.

"Because we recognized the guy following us. He was one of the officers who'd responded to the firm's initial burglary call."

"You're sure?" He stared at Kate with unblinking intensity.

Nodding, the paralegal leaned forward, her hands flat on the table. "William's death was no accident. I think he was killed because he was going to present the results of Dr. Sutton's stud—"

The sound of breaking glass interrupted her.

Gina looked at the table as her coffee cup exploded, splashing warm liquid over her hand.

What was happening?

"Down, Adam. Get down," shouted Harlan.

Kate slumped forward and Gina froze, unable to process what she was seeing. Everything seemed to move in slow motion.

Harlan dove over the table and grabbed her shoulders, crushing her into the vinyl seat before rolling her to the floor. Her cheekbone and temple rapped against the foot of the table base with a resounding thwack. More glass shattered and a loud thump echoed from the bench where her back had been a split second before.

Eerie quiet followed.

Harlan spoke calmly to her and Adam. "Stay down."

His breath stirred the hair beside her ear, and goose bumps rose along her arms.

Adam lay on the floor in front of her, crammed next to the center pole of the table, clutching his stuffed dinosaur. He nodded slowly.

Harlan rolled over her, and Gina's face mashed hard into the linoleum. Unable to breathe or move, she bit her lip against the sharp twinge in her cheek as his body covered hers.

"What's going on?" she gasped.

A woman screamed, and several other people began shouting.

"Someone's shooting at us," explained Harlan. His voice sounded laid-back, as if he were describing the weather, despite the chaos erupting around them. "Stay down."

"But why would—" Then she knew. God, maybe Kate Brooks wasn't so paranoid after all.

"What about Kate?"

Harlan raised up on his elbow, and for a moment Gina could breathe again. She turned her head. Adam was staring at her, his eyes wide with fright. She tried to smile encouragement but doubted her expression was little more than a grimace. Pain darted along the right side of her face.

Harlan leaned back down, keeping his weight on his elbows and his lips next to her ear. His breath on her left cheek was warm and oddly sensual, but his words were chilling.

"Kate's dead."

Chapter Five

Harlan slid out from under the relative safety of the table and landed in chaos. A screaming woman and crying restaurant patrons pushed toward the exit en masse. He narrowly avoided being trampled by a large waitress. With a final admonishment for Gina to stay put, he raised his head up over the debris-covered tabletop.

Kate Brooks was lying on the pages Adam had been coloring earlier. The paralegal stared straight at him. Her irises were already clouding. On the papers, blood mixed with orange crayon, making it appear as if the *T. rex* was bleeding.

But Harlan was eye level with the entry wound. There was no need to check her pulse. The back of her skull was gone.

Three neat holes marred the window, and two large chunks of stuffing hung out of the booth seat. The shooter had been after more than just Kate Brooks. If Harlan had been a split second later in tackling Gina, she'd be lying on that table as well.

He heard squealing tires and cautiously stood just in time to see a battered white pickup peeling rubber out of the parking lot. The vehicle was too far away for him to catch a license plate or anything that bordered on a description. He bent back down under the table.

What the hell was he going to do now?

Adam didn't need to see Kate. Harlan wasn't wild about

seeing her himself, and he'd been in this position more times than he cared to count. He had no idea how Gina would react, but he was getting them out of there now.

People were still shouting, although the initial chaos was calming. The restaurant was almost empty. He got down on his knees and peered under the table. Adam was rocking slowly back and forth holding tight to Dickens. Gina spoke softly to him while she continually patted his knee.

Harlan conjured up his poker face as he gave a big smile.

"Adam, we're going to play a game. I want you to close your eyes and keep them closed while I take you out from under the table. Okay? We'll have a treat when we get in the car, but no peeking. Got it?"

The boy's eyes were huge as he nodded. Harlan looked at Gina, "Can you get out once I have him?"

She nodded too.

"Okay, Adam, here we go. One, two, three, close 'em."

The boy obediently squeezed his eyes shut, and Harlan pulled him into his arms. Gina followed, holding her purse and clutching the papers she'd been looking at a few moments ago. They walked out of the restaurant as Harlan spoke softly to Adam, encouraging him not to peek.

Gravel crunched underfoot on their way across the parking lot. He didn't stop talking until they reached the car. Depositing Adam in the backseat, he was careful to face the boy away from the restaurant before telling him to open his eyes.

"Good job, big guy."

"Treat?" asked Adam, rocking back and forth on the seat.

"You betcha." Harlan rummaged in the console to retrieve a semi-melted chocolate bar that had been tossed there several days before.

Handing the candy to Adam, he looked up to see Gina swaying slightly beside the car. Shock and horror reflected dully in her eyes. She'd obviously looked at Kate on the way out.

Her complexion was ghostly pale except for the fiery-red

mark that ran from temple to cheekbone. No doubt she was going to have quite a shiner in a few days.

Harlan stood, gently leading her to the other side of the vehicle. He opened the door and guided her toward the seat.

"Sit down," he ordered, kneeling beside her when she did.

A thin sheen of tears glazed her eyes and gathered at the rims of her lids. She began to shake, breathing in short, shallow gasps of air.

"Put your head between your knees so you don't hyperventilate." He put his hand on the back of her neck and pressed forward. Her skin was warm, almost hot to the touch.

"Breathe. Slowly."

She complied without saying a word, taking in deep gulps of oxygen until her shuddering gradually subsided. He kept his hand on her neck, her long hair teasing the back of his hand. He glanced at Adam happily devouring his candy bar in silence. Chocolate spread from ear to ear.

This would seem normal but for the dead woman fifty feet away and another very live one about to pass out in his car. What the hell was going on?

A prickling sensation crawled up his neck, and his blood chilled despite the warmth of the day. He recognized this feeling. He'd learned to trust it over the last five years, especially in Iraq. Something, besides the obvious, was seriously screwed up. What had he gotten himself into? This was not what he had expected. This was not what anyone had expected.

The sun shone hot on his back as he stood and scanned the area while keeping his hand on Gina. Diner patrons milled about in front of the restaurant. Their shock appeared to be wearing off.

When he looked back down, Gina was staring at him. He pulled his hand away, feeling as if he'd been caught doing something wrong. "We've got to decide if we're going to stay here or not."

She blinked. "What?" Her eyes were losing that faraway

look when Harlan heard sirens in the distance. Someone had called the cops.

"Are we staying to talk with the police?" he asked.

"Why wouldn't we?" Surprise echoed in her voice.

"Because something here is not right."

She looked at him as if he'd lost his mind. "That's obvious." Her voice was flat.

He took a deep breath. He could just get in the car and drive, but this would be easier if she were cooperating. He took another run at explaining, as patiently and as quickly as possible. Something that went totally against every instinct he had.

He was used to giving orders and following orders, no questions asked. Gina wasn't going to put any stock in that prickly feeling running down his spine. "The shooter wasn't just after Kate Brooks. He shot at you, too."

She looked blankly at him.

Dumping all this on her wasn't fair. She was still dealing with the shock of sitting next to someone who'd had her head blown off before her eyes. But they were out of time. The siren was getting louder; the patrol car would be screaming around the corner any moment now. If they didn't hurry, they were screwed. At this point cooperation was overrated.

"We're leaving." He slammed her door to punctuate the decision.

She shook her head. "I don't understand." He could read her lips through the window as he jogged to the driver's side of the car.

"We can't just leave," she stuttered. "Can we?"

"Sure we can." He turned the key and threw the transmission into reverse. "It's for the best."

"Why?" Confusion and concern clouded her eyes. She had a death grip on the door handle as if she was considering jumping from the car. He'd better talk fast and do a better job than he did last night explaining his profession.

"The phone call I had before the meeting with Kate was from Sergeant Turner. When they searched Sarah's house last night, they found drugs. A lot of them. He thinks she was dealing crystal meth on the side."

"What?" Indignation replaced the shock in her voice as she loosened her grip on the door handle.

There, that was better than the hopelessness that had been in her voice earlier. He sighed inwardly, thankful for small favors. "They found methamphetamines in her kitchen. Turner wants to talk with us. They're convinced her disappearance is related to some kind of drug activity."

That did it. Clear-eyed now and full of outrage, she turned to face him for the first time since he'd gotten her in the car.

"That's ludicrous. Sarah would never— My God, she'll hardly take aspirin when she has a headache."

"I understand. But someone is trying to make her look guilty of something." They were speeding across the parking lot toward the exit.

Gina shook her head as the siren's wail grew closer. "It doesn't make sense...unless—" She was almost whispering.

He waited for her to catch up and saw her eyes widen when she did.

"You think Kate Brooks was telling the truth, don't you?"

He nodded. "Yes."

"You think someone is after the study Sarah was doing?"

He nodded again.

She swallowed audibly. "Then we'd better leave before the police get here, right?" Her voice was stronger.

"Right." Harlan smiled ruefully as he pulled onto the highway going in the opposite direction from echo of the sirens. "I think it's best to be far away from here when someone decides we shot Kate Brooks."

GINA GAPED AT HARLAN, scarcely believing what he'd said. Surely no one would think that they'd killed Kate. There were multiple witnesses. Witnesses who saw them get in the car and leave after the shooting.

No.

Suddenly she had a horrible feeling that they'd made a serious mistake in leaving the scene. Harlan didn't look at her. He watched the road, his expression blank.

What in God's name were they doing?

She nervously balled her fingers into a fist and felt the papers she was still holding crumple in her hand. She studied the pages, desperate to block her last vision of Kate Brooks, face down in a pool of blood.

Not much of what she was reading made sense until she reached the last page. In the top corner, a notation had been made. Gina recognized Sarah's small, cramped script. *"Final report with M.D."*

Who was M.D.? And why had Kate been shot? Had she been killed because of what was in these pages?

Gina stole another glance at Harlan. His face remained impassive as he turned right and drove through town. She shook her head. Maybe they were both lunatics. This certainly qualified as insanity.

She looked over her shoulder at Adam. With a chocolate-smeared face, he rocked back and forth, staring out the window and clutching Dickens tightly in his arms. He didn't respond when she called his name. She wasn't sure if that was normal for him or if he was in shock.

She felt as if she was in shock as well. She had no idea where they were going or what they were going to do next.

The more distance they put between themselves and the diner the better. She knew that. But it didn't stop her from clenching her fists until her fingernails dug into her palms. She tried deep-breathing exercises from a long-forgotten yoga class she'd bailed on in college, willing herself to close her eyes.

Moments later—or perhaps it was hours—she woke with a jolt. Harlan was gone. The car was parked outside a roadside motel office with a flashing neon vacancy sign and a flamingo painted on the door.

She whipped her head around to find Adam asleep in the

backseat. His cheek rested against the window, his breath fogging the glass. Pulling her seat belt loose, she frantically grasped for the door handle as Harlan casually strolled around the corner of the cinderblock building.

She tried taking another deep-cleansing breath in an effort to calm herself, but that was useless. Her heart was racing at what felt like ninety miles an hour.

Harlan opened the door and smiled grimly, sunglasses and a baseball cap pulled down low over his eyes. "I thought we'd stop here and figure out what we're going to do next." He handed her a plastic bag of ice.

She stared at the ice pack for a moment in utter confusion.

"For your face. Not sure how much good it will do now, though."

"Oh." She nodded gratefully and put the bag to her sore cheek. The frigid temperature was a shock to her sleep-warmed skin, and she pulled the ice away before gingerly setting it against her temple.

Sitting up straight in the seat, she looked around at her surroundings. A no-tell motel, this place was obviously one that accommodated its patrons by the hour as well as the week. The *V* and the *N* were burned out on the vacancy sign, but she could see a parking lot behind the main structure. Even in her half-asleep, half-panicked state, she realized the advantage of that.

"You don't think we should go back to Starkville?" she asked.

He shook his head and climbed inside. "I'm not comfortable until I know what's waiting for us there. Let's talk to Turner again before we go back. What Kate said about seeing a policeman following Sullivan is worrisome."

"Worrisome?" She blew out a breath in a rueful laugh. "Harlan, you do have a way with words."

"Yeah, I've heard that before." He pulled the Jeep around to the back of the lot and parked on the other side of a storage shed. Someone would have to be looking for the car and come all the way into the lot to find it.

"Feeling paranoid?" she asked.

"Hell, yes. And if you're not, you got hit harder on the head last night than I thought." He stared at her a moment with that penetrating gaze, and she looked away.

Last night when she'd gotten to Sarah's house. A lifetime ago.

Harlan handed her the key, and she opened the motel door while he carefully reached in to lift Adam out of the backseat. Unfortunately the boy woke up and started to cry hysterically when Mr. Dickens slid out of his lap. She plucked the stuffed animal from the crushed gravel parking lot and thrust him back into Adam's fist before she dashed inside the room to pull back the covers on the bed. No way would she lie down on the bedspread in a place like this. She wasn't about to let Adam sleep on what she suspected was germ-ridden material, either.

The only light shone through the open door. A strong acid scent of bleach overpowered the reek of stale cigarette smoke. Gina found that mildly reassuring.

Harlan sat on the other double bed and rocked the sobbing boy in semidarkness. At first Harlan simply whispered to him as he rocked, but Gina had to stop herself from staring when the Marine started to hum. His voice was low and deep. The sound wrapped around her, lulling her into a stillness she wouldn't have thought possible a few moments before.

She turned on the motel fan to provide white noise and to shake herself out of the lethargy she felt stealing over her as she listened to the Harlan's voice. When Adam was asleep again, Harlan laid him on surprisingly clean sheets.

"He's regressing," said Harlan quietly. "The further away we get from his routine, the more difficult it's going to be for him."

He walked out to his vehicle and returned carrying a zippered canvas duffel bag and her purse. Her eyes widened as he pulled a small triangular-shaped nylon case from the duffel.

"I wouldn't want to leave anything out there that I was real attached to." He pointed toward the window. "There's no parking lot security."

"What's that?" She pointed to the nylon case, her sense of unease growing.

In reply, he turned on the television to a low volume and sat opposite her at the scarred dining table. A local news program was just starting.

"Harlan?"

He unzipped what she suspected was a gun case. Her stomach flip-flopped when she saw the shiny metal of a gun barrel, winking in the lamplight.

"I think we should call Sergeant Turner back."

He didn't answer her, and she watched in mesmerized dismay as he took the gun out and checked what she assumed was the ammunition clip.

"I don't know," he finally responded. "Something weird is going on with your sister's investigation. The drugs in her house. That doesn't make sense to anyone who knows her. We need to talk about this before we call him."

He slid the gun back into its case and went to the side of the bed to shove the case between the mattress and boxspring in a homemade version of childproofing.

"I still can't believe Turner thinks she was dealing drugs. Are you sure you understood him correctly?" asked Gina.

"That's wishful thinking on your part. And while I appreciate your wanting to pretend this isn't happening, that's not very helpful right now."

She felt the flush rise from her neck along with her temper. "Well, what exactly is helpful? Whipping out a gun?"

"What the hell is wrong with you, Gina?" His tone was mild, but that didn't hide the frustration behind his words. "Don't you get it? Your sister is missing. A woman just died after telling us she had evidence that would destroy one of the most successful pharmaceutical companies in this country. Yes, I sure as hell do want a gun—several, if I could get my hands on them. I think we're going to need them before this is over."

"I don't know you. I don't know anything about you, and I'm supposed to trust you?"

She knew she was responding to her own frustration and not

his words, but even that knowledge didn't stop her. "I can't do that." *I don't do that. I've never been able to do that.* Her hands were shaking, and she put them in her lap, hoping that Harlan couldn't see how unnerved she was.

"What exactly are your other options right now?" he asked, his voice still calm.

"I don't have any." *And that's what's driving me insane.* "But give me some time." Her voice rose a bit at this, and Adam stirred.

They both looked at the boy before Harlan turned back to her, ignoring her outburst as if it had never happened. "All right. We'll figure something out." He headed out the door and spoke over his shoulder. "I'm going to see if we can get a cot for Adam and grab something for us to eat."

Embarrassed, Gina nodded, feeling like a three-year-old being left to cool down after a temper tantrum. "Wait, please."

He turned back.

"I'm sorry. I know I must seem ungrateful. I do appreciate everything you're doing for me and Adam. I'm just… I'm not accustomed to it. This is all so overwhelming, and I know I'm in way over my head. It's just that I like taking care of myself. I've worked really hard learning how. I'm having a difficult time giving that up."

He studied her again with those fathomless gray eyes. "Gina, everyone needs help now and then. If now doesn't qualify for you, I don't know what would."

"I know. I need to practice graciously accepting help."

He nodded. "Okay. Let's work on that." He headed for the door again.

Adam rolled over in his sleep, and as she turned to check on the boy, she caught the scene on the television. She blinked and stared, unable for a moment to believe what she was seeing. A photograph of Adam with the words *Amber Alert* across the bottom of the screen.

"Oh my God," she whispered.

Harlan followed her gaze to the TV, and he turned up the volume slightly as the screen split to a photo of Gina—the one from her driver's license—and one of him. He was in uniform, his hair so short she would hardly have recognized him.

The newscaster barely contained his excitement as he reported. "Harlan Jeffries and Gina Rodgers are traveling with this child, Adam Sutton, and are wanted for questioning in the shooting death of Kate Brooks earlier today at Martel's Diner in Kosciusko. It is not known if they are still in the area."

Bile rose in the back of Gina's throat as Sarah's picture flashed on the screen and the reporter continued. "There is some conjecture that this family drama is all related to a drug deal gone bad and this woman, Sarah Sutton, a professor at Mississippi State University. Dr. Sutton disappeared two days ago. Jeffries and Rodgers are wanted for questioning in her disappearance as well."

Horrified but riveted, Gina watched Sergeant Turner being interviewed. He described the drugs found at Sarah's home and theorized that the college professor was manufacturing crystal methamphetamines in her lab at the school and selling them on the street.

Stunned, Gina sat at the table while Harlan turned the volume down and lowered himself into the chair opposite her.

"Well, I guess that answers the question about calling Sergeant Turner," he said, no hint of triumph in his voice.

"What are we going to do?" she murmured, shock still careening through her system.

"I have no idea." He caught her eye and shook his head. "But give me some time."

Chapter Six

"How in hell did they even find her? There's no way they could have known each other." The gray-haired gentleman shoved his chair back from the desk as the two young men in front of him shifted nervously back and forth on their feet. The older man couldn't have cared less about their unease.

The aide cleared his throat. "Sir, we have no idea. We have people working on it right now."

"People that are costing me an arm and a leg, I'm sure. Do they realize what this could mean if they put it all together?" He continued to stare at the aide as pain seared across his chest. *Damn it.* "This was never even supposed to be a possibility." He could hear the strain in his own voice.

"Yes, sir. I know that."

"It could ruin everything, everything. You do understand that?" He took a deep breath through his mouth to ease the pain.

"Yes. But that's not going to happen, sir." This from the impossibly young officer on the other side of the desk.

"How did Higgins miss the sister?"

The man in uniform could have been blushing, but the light in the room was too dim to tell. "She ducked, sir."

Judas Priest. She ducked. "Well, make sure that doesn't happen again, you understand me? Otherwise, we're done."

"Yes, sir." With heels practically clicking, both men turned and left the room.

My God, what a nightmare, and all when he was but a breath away from having it done. *But at what cost?*

He lifted the heavy crystal glass with a surprisingly steady hand and wondered what it would be like to throw it across the room instead of sipping the contents. Watching the Waterford shatter into thousands of silvered pieces would be somewhat satisfying, if only temporarily so.

He'd never considered this kind of complication at the beginning. Only the prize. He'd been a fool.

The pain hit again, a sharp and vicious stabbing sensation across his chest. He took a deep breath. The yoga exercises he'd been taught helped sometimes.

He had no worries about his heart. Doctors had checked that out thoroughly a while back. Panic attacks brought on by stress. No big surprise there. He refused to take the meds his internist prescribed.

Another deep exhale, and the crushing sensations began to subside. *Thank God.*

If he just could contain this one piece of information. He had a good start, but what an excruciatingly fine line. He had to keep the lid on things a little while longer.

He leaned his head back against the seat. It'd be all right. Another sharp stab in the vicinity of his heart surprised him. A completely different sensation from what he'd just experienced. He'd thought he was done grieving months ago.

He took a deep sip of the twenty-year-old scotch. The time for sorrow was long past. He raised the glass to a framed picture on his desk. Two young men in army fatigues posed in front of a jeep.

He had an ace up his sleeve, but he sure as hell wasn't going to use it unless absolutely necessary. He shook his head. It was never supposed to come to this. But they were too far gone to look back now. At this point he would do whatever was necessary to survive. He'd made that decision months ago as well.

And come next November, he planned on doing more than just surviving. The most prestigious address in the country was within his grasp.

This time he looked at the picture and smiled. What the boy didn't know wouldn't hurt him. At least for now.

GINA LOOKED AROUND the barren motel room, searching for something to take her mind off the insanity that had suddenly become her life. Harlan had left ten minutes ago for food, supplies and a disguise. He'd been vague on what that last entailed, but she was fairly certain she was about to become a brunette.

Watching television didn't interest her. Her fragile peace couldn't handle another surreal news report splashing their pictures all over the screen. She wanted something normal, mundane. She opened her bag for a nail file and came up with her cell phone. Surprisingly, she saw two bars and a voice mail icon.

She listened to the messages in reverse order. There were three calls from Sergeant Turner, one terse message from her boss, and two from Tammy, her assistant at Dixon Meyers, clearly in angst about the new dog food photo layout. For a couple of minutes she allowed herself to get lost in the everyday details of work.

There were messages from Harlan when he was trying to find her three days ago, then Sarah's voice. Gina looked at the screen. The message was recorded on Monday, the day she disappeared.

"Hey, girl, it's me." Sarah's husky contralto sounded the same as always. Gina could hear a country song in the background. "I'm on my way home from work and—"

There was a long silence filled only with Toby Keith singing about not being as good as he once was. Gina heard a deep intake of breath before her sister spoke again.

"I think I may have screwed up." Her voice was shaky. "Hopefully, this is nothing and I'm being paranoid, but just in case, I've sent you something in the mail."

There was another silence. Toby continued to lament the trials of growing older.

"I know this is going to sound crazy, like something in a bad movie, but if something happens to me, get the package to Senator Jordan Bell. It's very important. More important than anything but Adam."

Gina glanced at the child still sleeping peacefully.

"I know you don't know him very well or understand him. But he's a great kid, Gina. He's sweet and dear. As long as you keep Dickens close, he's happy. Take care of him for me, okay?" She sniffed loudly.

"All right. I know we'll be laughing about this ridiculous message the next time—Well, hell, I'm being pulled over. A cop just appeared out of nowhere, and I'm not even going that much over the speed limit. Think I can talk my way out of it?"

Gina could hear the smile in Sarah's voice. Her sister had a remarkable talent for talking troopers out of tickets. It was one of the few family jokes told when they were growing up. Sarah never overtly flirted or did anything tacky, but inevitably she'd get off with a warning instead of the whopping fine Gina always managed.

Surely the police would have told them if there was a record of Sarah being stopped for speeding the day she disappeared. They hadn't mentioned it throughout any of the questioning the night before. The only explanation was frightening—there was no record because this hadn't been a routine traffic stop.

Gina's blood ran cold. The time stamp on the message was 8:36 p.m. Monday evening—about twenty minutes before Harlan had expected her home.

Sarah's voice was still cheerful and teasing. She had no idea what was about to happen. "I'll call you back and let you know. Love you. Talk to you soon."

Gina sat staring stupidly at the screen, imagining her sister pulling over and getting her wallet out to give the officer her license. She could see the smile Sarah used when she'd charmed traffic cops in the past, turning to face the officer, ready to talk about football or whatever topic came up.

Adam stirred and began to wake. Remembering Turner telling

them about the blood in the car, she crossed her arms over her middle. Her stomach clenched, and she tried to stop thinking, not wanting to imagine any more of what had happened next.

She had the presence of mind to hit the Save button and close the phone. The battery was almost dead.

What was she supposed to do now?

She leaned forward as she held her spasming stomach. Her imagination did not cooperate, flashing horrific pictures of what might have happened to Sarah at that traffic stop.

Adam rolled over and sat up, staring at her with wide owl eyes. "Hungy. Watch Maddie?"

He glanced around the room, looking for something or someone who obviously wasn't there, then dissolved into tears.

For a moment Gina considered giving in and crying along with him. Sarah's words came back to her. Dickens was on the bedside table. She squeezed her eyes closed against the stomach cramps and sat up straight to reach for the motel phone along with the stuffed animal.

"Yeah, well, what the hell happened?" Harlan pressed the phone to his ear and bit down on the inside of his cheek in an effort to control the angry torrent of words that was threatening to erupt. "A woman died in front of us, J.B. They almost killed Gina Rodgers, too."

"I don't know. I swear, Harlan, I don't." The reception crackled with static, but the man's conviction came through quite clearly, even from a thousand miles away.

"I'm not sure if I believe you."

"Come in, Harlan. I can protect the woman and the boy if you bring them to us."

"What about the damn Amber Alert? And you know as well as I do Sarah Sutton was no drug dealer."

"I know, it's a mess. Go to my attorney's house in Jackson. You know Carson. Turn yourself in there. He'll take care of everything. This has all been a huge misunderstanding."

"Misunderstanding, my ass. Kate Brooks is dead! That's a hell of a misunderstanding."

There was a long silence. Harlan thought he'd dropped the call, then realized J.B. had simply changed tactics. "It can't be good for the boy to be in this situation. Where are you?"

"Adam is fine, and I'm not telling you where we are. Not until I know what's going on first. This is not what we discussed. It was a very bad scene." He spit the words, biting back the expletives he would have preferred to use. "I don't trust you right now."

"I'm the only one you *can* trust to get you out of this." J.B.'s voice was calm, reasoning. They might have been discussing a change of dinner plans.

Harlan had to force himself not to press down on the accelerator. He was beyond losing his temper. He hadn't meant to leave Gina and Adam alone this long. Time had gotten away from him.

"Yeah, well, I'm not so sure about that. You've already lied to me once." He turned into the parking lot on two wheels. The sun had set an hour ago. "I've gotta go."

He clicked the end button to cut off the sputtering protests. With barely contained fury, he yanked the headset off his ear. This was not what he had signed up for. Not at all how things had been explained to him.

Damn it, he'd sworn he'd never be in this position again. But like it or not, he owed J.B. Some debts could never be repaid.

He was out of the car, balancing one bag on his knee and reaching for the sack of takeout when he heard Adam scream. Tossing both bags back into the vehicle, he raced for the room and pushed open the door to find what amounted to a domestic war zone.

Sheets and blankets had been ripped from both beds and lay in piles on the floor. One dresser no longer contained its drawers. One of the curtains had been pulled down and was hanging precariously by a single curtain hook. Both of the dining chairs were on their sides, and towels were scattered around the room. In the middle of the chaos, Adam paced back and forth wearing a path between the two beds and the bathroom. With only one shoe on, he was flapping his arms like mad and screeching every third step.

Gina was sprawled on the floor beside the door where she'd been pushed out of the way by Harlan's sudden arrival. Her face was tear-streaked, but there was a determined look in her eyes. She didn't say anything. Harlan stepped over her and stooped down to help her up. Her hands were shaking as he pulled her to her feet.

"Are you okay?" he asked.

She shook her head. "I need a minute," she said, walking out of the room and shutting the door carefully behind her.

Harlan didn't have to ask what had happened. He knew. Adam had had one of his infamous meltdowns. It had been a while since his last, and even then it had been related to a medication change. Harlan chalked this unhappy experience up to the stress and uncertainty of the past seventy-two hours.

Poor Gina. It was pretty scary to watch Adam go from sweet and compliant to demon child. Harlan had seen the transformation himself only once before, and he'd had a hard time believing his eyes at the time. It had been like flipping a switch.

He left Adam to continue his stimming and pacing as he straightened the room. The boy generally did better when left to work frustration and anger out on his own, rather than being interrupted. At least that was the way it had worked the one other time he'd seen this happen.

Harlan remade the beds, refolded the towels and was just getting the curtains back up on the rod when there was a brisk knock at the door. He glanced out the window and groaned inwardly before turning off the overhead light, pulling his cap down low and answering the summons.

"Yes?" he asked, opening the door just a fraction.

It was the manager who'd taken extra cash in exchange for not seeing his license earlier. "Everything okay in there?" The man's voice was laden with suspicion as he tried to peer into the room.

Not wanting to risk upsetting Adam anymore, Harlan stepped outside to finish the conversation. "Yeah. We're fine."

"Well, one of my other guests complained, said he heard a woman or a child screaming. I just wanted to make sure everything is all right."

"It's fine, really."

The manager still didn't look happy. 'Course, "happy" probably wasn't in his repertoire. Harlan decided he was going to have to spin a little to get the guy off his back.

He looked both ways before leaning down conspiratorially and explaining, "It's my wife. She's got a temper and well...she and the boy got into it. They're both okay. She doesn't hit or anything, just yells like a banshee. But when you get them both yelling... Whew. I'm sorry we disturbed your other guests. I'll make sure we keep it down."

The man's eyes narrowed, but he looked more satisfied with this answer than Harlan's earlier declarations of well-being. "Well, you do that. I don't want any more disturbances or you'll have to leave." The man nodded emphatically and stomped back down the sidewalk to his office.

Harlan cracked the door so he could see Adam as Gina walked out of the shadows.

"So I'm the yeller, huh?" Mascara ringed one eye and her nose was red. She'd obviously been weeping out here alone.

"I'm sorry. It was the only explanation that I thought would get him off our case. I know what really happened."

Gina studied him. The yellow light from beside the motel door was attracting moths. The tiny bugs flitted behind her head, landing on the door.

"God, that was incredibly hard. He started crying for you and Maddie and saying how hungry he was. I tried to talk to him, and when that didn't work, I thought I'd go to the vending machine down by the office, but I didn't have any change or singles. I couldn't go *into* the office because of the news reports, and after that I couldn't do anything right." She wiped her fingers under her eyes and succeeded in swiping mascara further across her cheek.

"The crying got worse, and when I tried to calm him down,

he went completely ballistic. I figured the only thing I could do was keep him from hurting himself and getting out of the room."

He nodded. "You're right. That's all you can do when he goes off the cliff like this."

"How often does it happen?"

"Couple times a month. The tantrums have been coming less and less. Sarah thinks they're usually related to a med change or illness. This one has gotta be because of the stress of the past three days. Getting out of his regular routine just overloaded him."

She glanced at the door, a wariness in her eyes he hadn't seen before. "Will it happen again?"

He shrugged. "I can't be positive, but I doubt it. He's generally pretty stable after an outburst, or at least that's how it's worked in the past."

Gina nodded and ran a steadier hand through her hair. "Okay, that's what I'll hope for then." Her curls caught the light and Harlan was reminded of the bags in his Jeep.

"That reminds me. I brought you something." He headed toward the car to retrieve the grocery sacks.

"Yeah? Oh, sorry. Wait. I can't believe I forgot to tell you this."

She pulled out her cell phone. "While you were gone, I retrieved my voice mails. Sarah left me a message on her way home Monday night. You need to hear it."

With a sick feeling unfurling inside him, Harlan listened to the message three times before handing the phone back to Gina. Damn, nothing made sense. He hated being lied to. And what he'd been told had just been turned upside down.

"Do you think she's alive?" She'd been staring at him as he'd listened.

"You've got to think positive here, Gina."

"Come on, Harlan. After everything that's happened today?"

"Let's be realistic. Do you really think she's alive?"

"I...I don't know."

She blew out a deep breath. "Thank you."

His brows knit in a question.

"For being honest." She continued. "For not saying it's going to be okay when we both know this is a disaster on so many levels. Thanks for not denying that."

He huffed a surprised laugh. "You're welcome, I think."

"We need to get Sarah's package," she said. "The study could be in it."

"That means going to Dallas," he cautioned.

"Right."

"Traveling with an APB and Amber Alert out for Adam."

"I know. Not ideal circumstances. But Sarah said it was important, and if she's not able to get this information to Senator Jordan Bell herself, I need to do it for her."

"There's no way I can talk you into letting me go and do this?"

"And have you leave me and Adam here by ourselves? I don't think so." She shook her head. "No way I can take care of him by myself. And after today, I'm not too proud to admit it. He might be fine over the next few days, or he might not. I don't want you four hundred miles away when I find out he's not."

Her ferocity surprised him. "What's changed? What's made you decide to do this?"

"Being in that room with Adam tonight. Waiting on you while he was coming apart at the seams, I realized that this was what I could do for Sarah right now. The only thing I'm capable of doing right now.

"She may be... I'll just say it, she may be dead. And Adam is— Well, I don't know what I can do for him now or ever. But getting this package to Senator Bell is what I can do for my sister. Right now, it's the only thing I can do for her."

He ignored the problem of getting the package into Jordan Bell's hands and focused on the immediate issue first. "I still think our moving around is a bad idea."

"Yes, I know. You've said that. But we're not going to solve anything sitting here in this motel room with that manager popping down here every time Adam squeals."

Arguing with her seemed pointless. "Speaking of which, let's get inside and eat before we attract any more attention."

She gave him a long, measured look. "All right. But we're not done talking yet."

Harlan gave what he hoped would pass for a bemused shrug and followed her inside. Adam's meltdown had apparently brought Gina out of shock with a vengeance.

The boy was still pacing but willing to wash his hands, and he came to eat with little prompting, as if the storm that had raged an hour earlier had never happened. Gina turned the television to a soothing satellite music channel.

An hour ago Harlan would have tried to talk Gina out of going to Dallas. But given the phone call he'd had on the road and Sarah's voice mail, it seemed the next logical step. Unless they were going to turn themselves in, and that wasn't a palatable option.

He'd seen the set of Gina's jaw when they were outside. He'd be wasting his breath to try to talk her out of retrieving Sarah's package. Right now, he wanted that material as much as she did. He hoped it could answer their unexplained questions.

Of course, there was no reason to tell Gina tonight of his interest in the package. She had enough on her plate. And getting out of the immediate area was a very good idea given the circumstances. So instead of arguing, they all ate, accompanied by the soft sounds of smooth jazz.

When Adam was done with his chicken strips, he came and crawled in Harlan's lap, resting his head on his shoulder. Gina watched them from across the table with a look of disbelief. Harlan knew what she was thinking. How could this be the same child?

He leaned down to make eye contact with the boy. "How about a bath, big guy? I think it's almost your bedtime."

Adam gave a noncommittal nod.

Gina looked doubtful. "Should we bathe him? He looks so peaceful. I hate to disturb him."

Harlan nodded. "It's part of his usual routine. Keeping a

schedule is one of the most important things we can do for him right now."

He motioned to the Wal-Mart bags beside the table. "I bought some pj's so we could get him cleaned up and into his regular bedtime gig." He stood with the boy in his arms and rummaged in a sack for a moment, gathering bath supplies. "You might want to get started on your hair if we're going to be on the road first thing in the morning."

The expression on her face was priceless as he dropped the box of haircolor in her lap on his way to the bathroom with Adam.

Hotshot red.

HARLAN TOOK A DEEP breath, inhaling particles of sand. Smoke burned his lungs as he tightened the tourniquet around Jimmy's leg.

"I'm so cold, H. So cold."

"I know. But you're gonna be okay. Just hang on."

"Save someone you can. I'm not going to make—"

Jimmy gasped as Harlan applied pressure to the leg wound.

"Screw that. I'm saving you." Harlan pulled another shirt out of his pack to absorb the blood and looked at Jimmy's face. There was a smile on his friend's lips, but his eyes were clouding over.

Hot tears rolled down Harlan's cheeks as he frantically began CPR compressions. Blood seeped through his clasped fingers.

"Don't you go like this, man. Not like this. I can't go back and tell them this, Jimmy. Don't make me tell them this."

"Harlan, Harlan."

He swam through the mists of a dream, Jimmy's dying words echoing in his mind. "*Save someone you can.*"

"Harlan."

Desert sand and acrid smoke disappeared. Soft hands were on his arm, shaking him awake and he startled. He rubbed palms down his face. He realized his cheeks were dry as he looked into Gina's eyes.

He'd been dreaming. Reliving a nightmare.

Gina was sitting beside him, leaning over him. Her new dark red curls brushed his cheek and shoulders. "Are you okay?"

He couldn't speak.

The light between the beds was on, but he couldn't see her face clearly. He'd been asleep on the floor. Neither of them had wanted to risk waking Adam by sleeping with him.

"Harlan, are you okay?"

He shook his head as he stared at her, struggling to ground himself in the present. Thinking of nothing beyond banishing the sight of Jimmy dying before his eyes again, he pulled her into his arms.

The smell of hair color and motel soap filled his senses, overpowering the smell of blood and smoke remaining from his dream. She wore a T-shirt from his workout bag that fell to her thighs revealing long legs, soft curves and bare skin.

He was holding her as she touched his shoulder, murmuring barely coherent but consoling words. "It's all right. You're awake now. It's okay." She touched his face, his hair.

He needed to let go of her. That thought registered as his grip tightened around her waist.

She stopped talking.

Her hair tickled his ear. Her breath on his cheek was soft. He pulled back and saw her eyes filled with concern. Despite the ice, her right eye and cheekbone were starting to bruise. For just a minute he wondered what would happen if he didn't let go of her now.

A very foolish, fleeting thought.

He sat up so fast that he rapped his head on the bedside table. "Sorry." He scooted away from her as he pulled the sheet around his waist. "I'm okay. Bad dream."

She smiled, concern for him still evident and apparently totally unaware of the effect she was having on him. "That's all right. You sure you're okay?"

As long as you let me hang on to you, I'll be fine. Instead he said, "I will be."

Adam rolled over with owl eyes and peered down at them. "Time wake up?" he asked.

Harlan glanced at his watch. It was 4:37 a.m.

He looked at Gina and forced himself to meet her eyes without looking away. "What do you think?"

She nodded. "Might as well get an early start."

"Time wake up?" Adam repeated.

Harlan nodded. "That's right, buddy. We're outta here."

Chapter Seven

Gina tried not to stare as Harlan stretched his back against the rest stop picnic table. It was difficult to ignore the rippling muscles as he worked out kinks in his neck and shoulders. The T-shirt he wore tightened across a well-toned torso and, she suspected, a killer set of six-pack abs. She hadn't been immune to that sculpted chest earlier when he'd held her against him.

This morning when she woke him from the nightmare, he'd clung to her like he wanted to inhale her. If he hadn't stopped himself, would she have kissed him? For a moment she imagined his lips on hers.

The texture. The taste. The feel of his breath on her skin.

A Mediterranean limbo jangled, interrupting her wandering thoughts. She scrambled to check the caller ID and had to clear her throat before she could look up at him and ask, "It's my office. Can they trace it if I answer?"

Harlan stopped midstretch and looked at her before answering. "Keep it short just in case."

"It's probably my boss calling to fire me…again." Starting to regret that universal charger she'd bought earlier at the truck stop, she flipped open the phone. "Hello?"

"Gina, thank God you answered. It's Tammy."

"What's going on?"

"Shouldn't I be asking you that? Your picture is all over the news. The police are here talking to us about your work, and Clay's about to have a conniption fit. Are you okay?"

Gina mentally crossed her fingers. "I'm fine, really. It's not as bad as it seems." A little voice inside her head mocked her. *No, it's worse.* "Tammy, you said the police are there right now?"

"Yeah, I'm holed up in our office with the door closed. They just got done questioning me about our 'association.' They make it sound like you're Bonnie of Bonnie and Clyde."

Gina swallowed the lump rising in her throat. Her carefully crafted career, her reputation, her life—everything was going up in smoke and all within less than twenty-four hours. She took a deep breath.

Dr. Phillips, her psychologist, was going to have some work to do when this was over. She was definitely thinking of herself as Gina the Screwup again. That innocuous thought should have made her smile, but the reality of it was frightening.

She forced herself to concentrate on the conversation. "Tammy, have they gone through my papers yet, my incoming mail?"

"Yeah, they did that first thing. They cleared off your desk and cleaned out your mailbox."

"Did they get the incoming FedEx stuff, too? Remember, the stuff that's been there a couple of days under the drafting table?"

"Let me check." Tammy was back a moment later. "That's weird, but no, they didn't take it. There are a couple of packages from Weathersbee Photo and a FedEx with a return label from—" Her voice dropped. "Sarah."

Thank God.

"That's great. Look, I really need that package. Where can I meet you to get it?"

"I don't know." Tammy's voice took on a strained quality that had alarm bells going off in Gina's head. "This isn't some kind of drug thing, is it? The police were pretty insistent that we let them know if you contacted us."

"Tammy, you know me. You know I didn't do what they're saying. Sarah's not involved in drugs, either. Please, meet me with the package. I'll tell you everything I know." Gina took a deep breath before continuing. "And after that, if you're not convinced, you can call the police yourself."

There was a long pause. For all her naïveté, Tammy was not a pushover, and Gina didn't know what else to say, so she waited for her assistant to speak.

"God, you're right, of course. Where are you now?"

"We're a couple hours outside of Dallas. We can meet you wherever you say or even pick you up in front of the building downtown."

Tammy hesitated. "I've lost so much time today with the police, I can't take a lunch. Why don't you meet me in the lobby at five-thirty?"

Now it was Gina's turn to hesitate. "I can't come inside."

"All right. Just park out front and call me when you're here."

Something about this didn't sound right, but Harlan was motioning for Gina to wrap up the call. She'd talked longer than she'd planned. "Okay, I'll talk to you in a couple of hours. And, Tammy, thank you for trusting me."

"Of course I trust you." Gina could feel the strain across the cell line and closed the phone feeling distinctly uneasy. Harlan was staring at her.

"What did she say?"

"The police have been there spewing their poison about us. They've taken everything from my work space, but she has the package from Sarah. Miraculously they missed it."

He raised an eyebrow in question.

"Our mail system leaves much to be desired."

"Huh. You sure you trust her?" He didn't seem to be judging but really asking.

She started to answer, "Yes, of course." Then stopped herself. "A week ago I would have said I absolutely trust her. But now I'm not so sure. So, no, not entirely. Not that I have any other options at this point." She told him about meeting Tammy after work.

Adam had been chasing butterflies and was now happily digging in the dirt with Dickens seated beside him.

Harlan watched her intently as he listened. "Maybe we do have some options. But I think we need to get moving, just in case Tammy isn't as trustworthy as you'd like to think." He called to Adam.

"Harlan, with our pictures all over the news and the police knowing our car, are we safe still driving your Jeep?"

"Well, yeah, I think so."

"They are looking for this Jeep, aren't they?"

"Not anymore."

"I don't understand." She looked at him, then looked at the bumper.

"I swapped license plates with a truck last night at Wal-Mart. I'll do it again tonight sometime. We should be safe for a bit longer."

As Gina climbed in the front seat, she didn't dwell on the fact that he'd known to swap plates eighteen hours earlier. But she couldn't ignore her concerns about Tammy.

She turned and studied Harlan.

"What if Tammy changes her mind and decides she doesn't want to give the package to me or goes to the police? She didn't sound entirely convinced."

Harlan's gray eyes met hers. "Well, then we'll have to convince her that we're *trustworthy*." The way he said trustworthy made Gina uncomfortable.

"But how? I mean, we can't hurt her."

"No, but we can be persuasive."

Gina knew she wasn't hiding the look of revulsion on her face. Harlan didn't seem to notice.

"You were asking earlier about how I did my job. This is part of it. You turn off the emotions and you just do it."

"You're talking about being cold and manipulative."

"No, I'm talking about survival. From now until this is over, that's how you need to think about things too. Your sister said the package was important. You said you'd do anything to get it. This is what is required to get the package."

He pulled onto the highway as she digested that, wondering exactly when in the past forty-eight hours she'd gone from being a friend to being Machiavellian. Probably shortly after she'd gone from being a businesswoman to being a felon.

Dr. Phillips was still on her speed dial, and it was a good thing. If she survived this, she was going to need him. She'd been wrong earlier. She'd leapfrogged right over screwup and gone straight to criminal.

"THE EFFICACY OF THIS particular vaccine has never been in question," stated the president of PharmaVax. He spoke boldly into the microphone on the table in front of him.

"But there have been instances of adverse effects, have there not?" asked Senator Hall from Texas. She was seated at a rounded dais above him. Her accent was thick.

"Yes," admitted the pharmaceutical executive.

"How many?"

"I don't have the exact numbers in front of me."

"Excuse me, sir, isn't that the whole reason for the existence of this committee?" Sandra Hall indicated the men and women seated beside her. "Isn't that the whole reason you are here today testifying before us?"

Senator Jordan Bell leaned back in his leather seat, barely suppressing his grin. Sandra was up for reelection and playing to the network and C-SPAN cameras in the gallery. PharmaVax president Robert Johnson looked like a deer caught in headlights.

God, hadn't anyone at PharmaVax prepped the man for the questions he would get today? If they wanted a liability waiver, they were going to get a few questions about adverse reactions from their past vaccines. This was not the day for being unprepared.

Sandra ignored the man's discomfort. "Sir, as I understand it, your company wants a liability waiver for the new H3N6 vaccine you are developing for the Indonesian flu. Now, I know the media and everyone else is real scared of this new virus. And they should be. It's got a 95 percent mortality rate. But before we discuss giving PharmaVax a free pass on liability for your new 'miracle vaccine,' I've got some questions about the adverse reactions your other vaccines have caused in the past."

She proceeded to grill the man, but he took it well, and ten minutes later Jordan saw why Robert Johnson was CEO and president of PharmaVax.

He stared directly at Sandra Hall. "Human error is part of the manufacturing process. There is no way around it. Is that loss acceptable? No, of course not. But is it something that will happen again?

"Unfortunately yes, and while the particular error we discussed today will not recur, something else we haven't thought of will. We try to think of every conceivable thing that could go wrong, but there's always that one thing that you don't ever dream of. That's why we need a liability clause."

"To cover your company's lack of imagination?" she asked.

Robert Johnson smiled, completely at ease. "No, ma'am. To stop a pandemic. No one else in the world is as close as we are to finding an Indonesian flu vaccine. All other companies are at least three years away. But we know the virus is coming. Soon."

Johnson leaned forward in his seat, earnest in his argument. "Lawsuits and the threat of lawsuits are slowing us down. In some cases, involving things we had nothing to do with. We're worried that we're running out of time."

"So you want to take shortcuts?" asked Sandra.

"No, ma'am. I'm not talking about shortcuts. I'm talking about being reasonable. We can finish production and have a viable product to market in time to stop this virus. But we can't do it if we are dragged into court at each and every turn by a tort system gone mad."

He looked at each member on the dais as he spoke. "The question for this committee is should the threat of lawsuits keep us from finding the answer to the pandemic that's coming."

Cameras rolled and the evening news had their sound bite. Jordan Bell listened as the rest of the senators asked their questions, but none came close to derailing the executive. Critics could talk about the astronomical pharmaceutical profits and how they were raping the American public, but the bottom line was simple.

No one wanted to be responsible for shutting down the company that could save the country from the next worldwide pandemic.

Chapter Eight

Gina watched Harlan walk into Chase Tower, home of Dixon Meyers Advertising. He seemed to melt away from the vehicle and into the mass of people crowding the sidewalk. She couldn't get over the dramatic change in his appearance. How ordinary he looked.

It was definitely something in his posture. He hunched his back or did something he didn't normally do. Wearing a baseball cap and wraparound sunglasses, suddenly he was invisible. He'd said no one would notice him, but she hadn't really believed him until now.

She slid over the console and tried dialing Tammy again. Where was the woman?

She shifted around in her seat to get comfortable. Crawling over consoles was not part of her athletic repertoire. She was to wait with Adam in the car while Harlan retrieved the package, and to call, if there was a problem with their ten-minute loading and unloading parking space—the only spot available this afternoon in downtown Dallas.

In the backseat, Adam put aside his Chicken McNuggets.

"Need go potty." His voice was quiet but insistent.

He didn't, Gina thought. He couldn't. They'd gone before they left the fast-food restaurant. She closed her eyes and gritted her teeth.

"Can you wait just a minute, Adam? Harlan will be back, and he can take you."

"Gotta go now!"

Gina looked around. What was she supposed to do? She and Harlan hadn't talked about this possibility. *Crap.* No, not crap. Don't even think that. She let out a short breath when she spied a Subway restaurant across the street.

She weighed the pros and cons of leaving the car.

"Go now!" insisted the small voice.

The pros won. "Okay, Adam, here's what we're gonna do. We're going across the street to that Subway and use their restroom."

"'Kay."

She crawled over the console again, grabbing the keys and her purse along the way. At the last minute she thought about a disguise and planted sunglasses on her nose and one of Harlan's spare baseball caps on Adam's head. They waited at the cross-walk, with Adam holding himself and dancing a jig. "Can't wait."

Gina's voice took on a steely calm.

"Yes, you can. We're almost there."

Businessmen and women looked at them. A mother and son on an excursion in downtown Dallas at five-thirty on a Friday was not a common sight and a lousy idea, but a young boy needing to go potty qualified as an emergency pretty much anywhere in civilized society. The light turned and the crowd of pedestrians crossed like cattle. Gina suppressed the urge to shove people out of the way.

Beside her, Adam whimpered. "Gotta go."

"I know, baby. Almost there."

They hit the door of the Subway and raced to the bathroom only to be met with a locked door and a sign that read, Restrooms Are for Customer Use Only. Please See Manager for Key.

Gina barely managed to keep from screaming as she went to the register to request the key and whatever she had to buy to get it. A small television on the counter was tuned to the evening news, and the clerk was nowhere to be seen.

A newscaster was reporting on the Vaccine Safety Congressional hearings as Gina shouted and rang the bell by the cash register. A pimply teenager moved like molasses from the backroom and insisted on taking her order before finally handing over the key.

"No!" Adam wailed.

Gina turned in time to see the darkening stain at the front of his jeans. His little face crumpled as he began to cry and repeat quietly, "Big boys don't wet, big boys don't wet, big boys don't wet."

It was the most complete sentence she'd ever heard him utter. But the blow to his self-esteem caused her heart to break. For a moment she was transported back in time, hearing herself mutter a similar litany about big girls not crying.

The clerk sputtered about not cleaning up the mess.

Gina shot the insensitive fool a venomous look, then gathered Adam in her arms, careful to avoid the damp spot as she hugged him close. "It's okay, baby. Everybody makes mistakes. Don't you worry. We'll fix you up in a jiffy."

Adam let her hold him but continued to mumble his mantra through the tears as Gina unlocked the door.

The cashier grew a heart and brought her some napkins without being asked and said he'd have her sandwich ready when they got out. Gina cleaned Adam as best she could, grateful for Harlan's Wal-Mart sack waiting in the car.

Harlan. Oh damn. She'd forgotten to call and tell him what was going on. When she did, she got his voice mail. She hung up and went back to washing her hands and wishing they sold tequila shots at Subway. Her cell phone rang as she was getting Adam dressed again. The caller ID showed it was Harlan.

"Where the hell are you?" he demanded.

"Adam had to go to the bathroom. We're at Subway."

"Well, get over here now. I think they're about to tow the car. It may be too late. See what you can do. Maybe you can explain your way out of it."

Gina gulped. "Did you find Tammy?"

"No, she's in a meeting and can't be disturbed. I came back

down to talk to you and saw security at the Jeep. You'll do better at talking your way out of this than I will. A woman with a child is much more sympathetic than a single guy in a hurry."

Gina sighed. "Okay. I'll try." She hurried out to the counter to pay for the sandwich she'd ordered to secure the bathroom key. The small television was still tuned to the news.

She was fumbling for change when Adam said "Mommy" and pointed to the TV.

Startled, Gina looked up. A photo of Sarah was on one side along with a live shot of Harlan's house and a body bag being rolled out on a gurney.

The lights seemed to dim, and Gina's fingers went limp on the coins in her hands.

The cashier looked at her strangely.

"Could you turn that up, please?" she asked. Her voice sounded hollow even to her own ears.

"Today police made a grim discovery in the disappearance of Dr. Sarah Sutton. Her body was found in the home of Harlan Jeffries—the man accused yesterday of abducting her son, Adam Sutton, along with her sister, Gina Rodgers. The Amber Alert has now been extended to the state of Texas, where Miss Rodgers is a resident. Police suspect they could be traveling there."

Pictures of Harlan, Adam and Gina flashed on the screen.

"It is not known at this time how Dr. Sutton was killed, only that her body was found in a shallow grave in the backyard of Mr. Jeffries' home due in part to an anonymous tip."

"Mommy?" Adam's voice had taken on a strange quality. "Mommy?"

Oh, Jesus. He'd just heard all that, too. Sarah was dead. How? When? And in Harlan's backyard?

"Turn it off, please," Gina said, not caring what kind of attention she was drawing to herself.

Adam began to whimper. "Mommy! Want Mommy!"

"Please, it's upsetting him. Turn it off."

She slammed her money on the counter, picked up Adam and ran out, leaving behind the sandwich and a very confused clerk. The wet spot on his jeans chilled the front of her T-shirt.

"Mommy!"

"I know, baby, I know. It's all right. It's all right." She got to the crosswalk on autopilot. Everything was numb except her heart. She felt as if a band were tightening around it and she couldn't breathe.

She looked across the street to their vehicle. Harlan was right. There was indeed a security officer and someone who appeared to be a tow driver. How was she going to get that car away from them without getting arrested and without being hysterical?

"Mommy! Want Mommy!"

"I know, baby, I know. I do, too."

Adam buried his face in her neck and clutched her hair. The pain and the horror were closing in on her, but she had to hold it together and see if she could wheedle her way out of this.

She sucked at talking her way out of this stuff. Sarah could do it. *God, Sarah. What had happened?*

She crossed with a group of pedestrians all giving her a wide berth with her weeping child. Adam had dissolved into inconsolable sobs and was wrapped around her, holding on tight. She squeezed him, plastering what she hoped would pass for a pleasant if harried expression on her face and walked up to the vehicle. The tow truck was a couple of cars behind, boxed in by traffic.

"Excuse me." She walked past the security guard and tow-truck driver, straight to the back passenger door.

"Hey, lady, you're not supposed to leave the car unattended. We're gonna have to tow you."

"Oh, I know, I saw the sign. But we had a little emergency here. My nephew had to go to the bathroom."

She unlocked the door and opened it, bending in to unclasp Adam from her neck and waist and put him in his seat. She stood, the wet spot from his jeans clearly visible on her dark T-shirt. The cool breeze and dampness made it obvious that she'd forgone a bra that morning. The security guard noticed. "Unfortunately, we didn't make it to the restroom in time."

The guard's face was now focused on her chest. Gina realized with startling clarity that this was what Harlan had meant about turning off your emotions and doing what you had to in order to survive. She'd crumble if she stopped to consider for more than a moment that she was letting a man ogle her breasts less than five minutes after learning her sister was dead.

She swallowed the bile rising at the back of her throat and turned what she hoped would pass for a smile toward the tow-truck driver. He looked mildly sympathetic to her plight.

Adam let out another wail. "Mommy. I want Mommy."

Gina bent down, making sure she let the security officer get an eyeful of her ass. "I know, baby, I know. It'll be okay."

"Lady, you can't put him in the car. We're about to tow it." This was from the security guy, although at this point he didn't sound nearly as forceful as he had a moment ago.

She turned back to face him and leaned an arm on the door to give him a better view and jiggled. "Well, I'm here now. So there's no reason to tow it. I'll just get out of your way and be on my way. We'll get this very unhappy camper home, and everything will be hunky-dory."

She smiled even as she felt the tears forming at the corners of her eyes. She blinked them away as she opened the passenger door and slid over the seat and console as if she'd been doing it for ages. From out of nowhere Harlan came jogging up and hopped into the passenger seat beside her.

"Sorry for the confusion," Harlan mumbled to the guard, snapping the door shut.

Finally in the sanctuary of the car, Gina felt the trembling start. She stared straight ahead as the security officer went ballistic and pulled out his radio.

The tow-truck driver started yelling. "Lady, we've already called the police. They'll be here any minute."

Her hands were shaking, but she ignored that, along with the yelling men, and jammed keys into the ignition.

"Get us out of here," said Harlan.

Still numb, she pulled into the traffic with a squeal of tires and nipped around a DART bus to join the wall of cars. Within four minutes they were headed north on Central Expressway. Gina concentrated on driving and breathing.

Adam continued to sob in the backseat. No one spoke.

They were passing LBJ Freeway when Harlan broke the silence. "What the hell happened back there?"

She didn't answer. She couldn't. She was still focused on driving and breathing. To add talking would be too much at this point.

Very slowly Harlan touched her shoulder. "Gina? What happened?"

She took a deep breath and whispered, "Sarah's dead." She didn't look at him as she said it, and he didn't answer.

Instead, he turned on the radio. The station was a classical one they'd found earlier that Adam liked. Samuel Barber's "Adagio for Strings" was playing. He turned the volume up.

"Pull over," he demanded.

"What?"

"I said pull over."

She didn't argue.

The next exit put them on the service road near an industrial park with a small greenbelt. She parked the car in front of a building that was for lease and laid her head on the steering wheel. Hot tears burned the back of her eyes, but she couldn't fall apart, not yet.

Big girls don't cry.

She sat up and turned to face him. "It was on the news at Subway. They found her body at your house. Anonymous tip."

His jaw tightened. She could see it in the waning light. She'd seen that look before when she'd questioned him about his work the first night they'd met. "Adam knows…something."

Harlan muttered a foul curse under his breath.

She flinched.

He squeezed his eyes shut for just a moment.

"The television. I didn't think until it was too—" Her voice broke. "Too late. And then you called, and I had to talk to those men."

She took a deep breath but couldn't get enough oxygen. "Oh, God. I cannot believe this is happening. It's just—" Her chest tightened. She bent over, gulping in air. The gulps turned to sobs as she cried for her sister, her nephew and herself.

Hot tears rolled down her cheeks, and her nose ran in torrents. She could taste the mucus and the salt as snippets of memories flashed before her eyes. Giggling late at night, secrets shared under covers with flashlights shining, laughter over the first disastrous forays into makeup, heated rollers, and of course boys.

Darker times, too. Voices raised, yelling and Sarah holding her hand. Sarah always there looking out for her. As long as Gina could remember. Who was going to look out for her now?

Oh, she could do it herself. She'd been doing it herself for some time. But in the back of her mind, she'd always known Sarah would be there to catch her if she fell.

And Adam. Her grief was nothing, nothing compared with his. What was going to happen to that boy now? Who was going to care for him?

Obviously her. But oh, God, her... The tears started afresh. The overwhelming pain and responsibility crushed her heart like a vise as the sorrow imploded. She hunched over the steering wheel and wept.

Chapter Nine

Harlan watched Gina for a moment, wishing he could hold her, ease her pain. But there was nothing he could do, except leave her alone.

He couldn't believe Sarah was dead. That her body had been found at his house was disturbing on so many levels. When was Gina going to start thinking about that?

Sooner than most people would, under the circumstances. And what was going to happen when she starting putting things together?

Adam's voice could be heard every once in a while over the radio and Gina's soft sobs. "Big boys don't wet, big boys don't wet."

Well, he could do something about that. Harlan got out of the car and opened the backdoor. Barber's "Strings" was still playing. "Come on, Adam, let's take a walk."

The boy didn't respond. He continued rocking and muttering. What was going to happen to Sarah's boy now?

Seeing that news report must have been a nightmare for Adam. He had been doing so well at potty training. At everything. The kid hated to make mistakes. Not even taking the emotional ramifications into consideration, an accident would have been enough to set him over the edge. Add to that seeing his mom's murder reported on the news, and there would be a real regression in the making.

They needed a place to decompress. Now. The question was where.

Harlan reached into the car and took Adam's hand. "Let's take a look at those britches." The spot was starting to dry, but the boy would have a rash if they didn't get him changed soon. "It's not too bad. We've got another pair of superhero underpants in back. You can change right here in the car."

He helped Adam into the final pair of clean underwear and jeans, noting that they'd have to find a laundromat or buy more clothes soon. One crisis at a time, he told himself. A laundromat was pretty far down the list of impending problems right now.

Gina was rifling through her purse. Harlan decided she needed privacy or as much space as he could give her to pull herself together. He got her a bottle of water from the cargo area. Adam continued rocking and mumbling, holding Dickens closely to his side.

What were their options?

Ditching his car was a priority after the incident with the security guard and the tow truck driver. The men might not put together who Gina was, but then again it was foolish to take chances.

He looked over at Adam as he rocked. They had to get him to a quiet place soon. As much as he hated it, he'd given Gina all the time he could. "Gina?"

"Yeah?" Her eyes were tear-stained but focused.

"I'm sorry, but we've gotta get out of here."

"I know. I've been thinking about that. We need to get rid of this car, don't we?"

The surprise must have shown on his face. He figured she'd be in too much shock to put that together. "Yeah, we need another vehicle."

"My car is at the airport. Would the police be looking for it yet?"

"That's a distinct possibility."

Her shoulders slumped as she held up a loaded key chain. "I was checking to see if I had the keys. Are these worthless now?"

Harlan felt himself smile for what felt like the first time all day. "No, I think we can work around the police for a little while."

"The license plate thing?"

He nodded and handed her the water bottle he'd forgotten he

was holding. "I'll drive us to the airport, and we'll figure out where to go from there." He started to get out of the vehicle.

"My apartment is definitely out, though, right?"

Harlan nodded again. "Even if they aren't watching it, the police have probably asked the management or someone there to notify them if anyone shows up. We can't take that chance."

"So we need a place that no one can connect to me or Sarah."

"Yes."

"What about Adam?" She continued to surprise him.

"What did you have in mind?"

"My family has an old lake house, very secluded. It's not in my name or Sarah's. My stepfather, Adam's grandfather, put it in a trust for Adam before he died, so it isn't in any of our names. I don't have a key, but I know how to get in. It's about an hour from here. Would that work?"

He couldn't imagine the police running down that kind of remote connection and staking it out within the next twenty-four hours. He nodded. "For a little while at least. I'll get us to the airport and your car. Then you can give me directions out to the lake."

He slid out of the backseat and walked around to the driver's door. As he opened the door, he looked back at Adam. "We need to get him settled as soon as possible. You say he's familiar with the place?"

She nodded her head. "Sarah spent quite a lot of time there. We were all out together at Thanksgiving." She stood, started toward the passenger side and stopped. She stared into the backseat. "Would it help if I sat with him?"

Harlan shrugged. "Why don't you try and see what happens?" He held the door as Gina slowly eased into the backseat beside Adam.

At first the boy didn't seem to notice her presence until she tentatively slipped an arm around his thin shoulders. Harlan couldn't tell she was holding her breath until she audibly exhaled. Adam stilled and leaned into the crook of her arm before beginning his litany and rocking again, this time in her arms.

With Beethoven playing softly on the stereo, Harlan put the vehicle in Reverse and pulled onto the service road, all the while watching them in the mirror. Gina rested her cheek on Adam's head and patted his arm. Tears clung to her eyelashes.

"Want Mommy," mumbled Adam.

"I do, too, honey. But it's all right," she whispered. "We're going to be all right."

God, I hope so, thought Harlan. *But I'm starting to have some serious doubts.*

Friday night

OLD GHOSTS FLITTED AROUND Gina as they drove the last two miles onto the lake house property. Ghosts of childhood trips there, of the good times with her parents and her sister, before those dark times after her mother's death. She hadn't told Harlan everything of her life, didn't figure he wanted to know all the gory details of her childhood.

He was cautious. Even though they'd swapped cars and license plates at DFW's long-term parking, Harlan pulled into the carport so her Honda was hidden from any casual passersby.

"Leave the headlights on for a minute," Gina instructed, climbing wearily from the car and searching the back patio for the key safe, exactly like the one Sarah had in her yard in Starkville. She felt a nauseating sense of déjà vu as she opened the frog and grabbed the key, which hadn't been used since the fall, when she'd locked herself out in the rain.

Gina stood paralyzed for a moment, frozen by the silly memory of all three of them—Sarah, Adam and herself—standing beside the frog trying to catch raindrops with their tongues. It was the last time she remembered laughing with Sarah.

Ruthlessly pushing aside the pain and sorrow, she turned to the car and raised the key in the headlight's glare. Harlan killed the engine and climbed out with a flashlight and the sack of groceries they'd picked up on the way.

Opening the back door, they were greeted with a mild musty scent. The place was what she'd always considered rustic but comfortable—three bedrooms with a living and dining area that led onto a balcony overlooking the lake. The back of the cabin was on stilts.

Harlan had Adam in the tub by the time Gina was done removing dustcovers from the furniture. She heard splashing in the big bathroom in the hall, but she didn't hear Adam's usual patter. He'd been equally withdrawn during the car ride.

She made up the twin beds in the room she and Sarah had shared years ago, then found Dickens among the plastic sacks and propped him up on one of the pillows in Adam's bed to stand guard. The scent of central heat turned on for the first time in a season filled the air.

She realized she was in shock only as exhaustion overwhelmed her. She sank into the big easy chair that had been in the living room for as long as she could remember and pulled a soft cotton blanket around her.

Sarah was really gone.

Memories washed over her. Summers spent catching bottles of fireflies and keeping them in their room at night. Watching the stars come out one by one. The smell of Noxzema on her skin after being sunburned on the lake. Laughing with Sarah and her mother and even her stepdad before that relationship went south. Tears slipped from the corner of her eyes as she let the emotions engulf her. Sitting in this chair brought back other memories. Some not so pleasant.

Her stepfather's deep voice. *"You're such a failure. You'll never amount to anything. You're just like your mother."*

She bit the inside of her cheek just like she'd done then.

"Big girls don't cry."

She sucked in a deep breath and wiped her face. She couldn't fall apart. Not now. Too much was left to figure out and be done. She closed her eyes and quit fighting the inevitable, drifting off to sleep with the sounds of splashing water in the background and wet tears on her cheeks.

HER RINGING CELL phone pulled her from sleep moments, or perhaps hours, later. She wasn't sure as she awoke, slightly groggy and disoriented. There was another blanket covering her hips and legs.

Harlan?

The shrilling tone shattered the temporary peace she'd found. She answered without looking at her caller ID. "Hello?"

"Gina, what the hell is going on?"

"Clay?" She sat up, trying to orient herself.

"What are you doing to me? To the firm?"

She could tell from the careful enunciation of his words that he'd been drinking. "Clay, this has nothing to do with you or the firm."

"My God. The FBI, the police? The clients are going insane at PharmaVax. They've pulled the account, thanks to you."

"But that's…" she stammered. Then she realized he didn't want explanations or empathy; he just wanted someone to chew on. And did she really care?

"I told them we could fix it. I fired the whole creative team. Told them we were starting fresh. But would they listen? No."

PharmaVax pulled the account because of her? That made no sense. Then she caught the rest of what he'd said. "You fired who?"

"The whole creative team. Jason, Tammy, the lot of 'em…. They have you to thank for that, Gina. Just thought you'd want to know."

Clay, you're such a jerk. "When?"

"What?" he mumbled.

"When did you fire Tammy?" She cared about the others too, but Tammy was her main concern right now—with that package from Sarah.

"This afternoon. Right at closing. Tammy was first. Hell, she had a FedEx package addressed to you in her briefcase. I sent that straight to the FBI. Security escorted her ass right out of the building. It wasn't pretty."

Gina stared at the phone. Unbelievable. "Clay, you really are a rat bastard. You and your ice-bitch wife deserve each other. You were lousy in bed, too."

She clapped her phone shut, fully awake now and furious. She probably shouldn't have made that last comment, but it was true. God knows he wouldn't have given her a job reference anyway. She snorted a tiny laugh and heard a noise behind her.

Turning around to see Harlan, she felt herself blush to the roots of her hair and smiled sheepishly. "Sorry about that. My mother always told me, 'If you can't say something nice, don't say anything.'"

"Funny, mine always said, 'If you can't say something nice, come sit by me.'"

She laughed out loud. "Did she really?"

He grinned. "Only after I was older and already on the road to hell. Less impressionable that way."

She chuckled as he settled in the recliner next to hers.

"Thank goodness. Who knows how you would have turned out if she'd said that while you were younger."

"Or who I'd have taken with me. You'd have liked her. She was a pistol."

She nodded. "I bet I would have, too. I don't remember a lot about my mother. She died when I was eight. I…I missed a lot."

She sobered and thought of Adam. All he would be missing. Instantly the pain was back. Overwhelming. Crushing.

"So it was just you and Sarah?"

"Yeah. And my stepdad."

Harlan listened without prompting or prying, and that—more than anything—made her want to tell him.

"When my mom died, my stepdad…" She stopped, took a breath and glanced down at her hands. When she looked up, he was staring at her with an intensity that had originally made her uncomfortable. Now she realized he was truly concentrating on what she was saying.

"I'm going to hate this part of your childhood, aren't I?"

She shrugged. "It was kind of a reverse Cinderella story."

He cocked an eyebrow. "What does that mean?"

"My stepdad really, really didn't like me." There was a world of pain in those words, but she didn't elaborate. It was over a long time ago.

A stricken expression crossed Harlan's face, but he didn't ask for an explanation.

She shook her head to answer the unasked question. "He never... He just hit me...a lot. He was a very angry man after my mother died. I think he was angry before she died, but he kept it under control better then. He tried to get my mom's family to take me, but my grandparents were older and not very healthy.

"Besides, Sarah wouldn't hear of it." She smiled sadly at the memory. "Sarah became my fairy godmother. She took care of me when nobody else..." Gina swallowed, her throat hurt from crying earlier. "I can't believe she's gone," she whispered.

Harlan put a hand over hers. The warmth was comforting. She leaned her head back to close her eyes. Her chest was tight and she couldn't speak. She took a ragged breath and then another. Harlan held her hand as the steel band across her heart eased. She was able to blink back the tears.

"How's Adam?" She opened her eyes again.

Harlan looked back down the hall. "Asleep for now. He didn't speak at all tonight. I don't think he understands exactly what's happened, but he's grieving in his own way. I don't know what he'll be like in the morning. He needs to see the psychologist that works with him. I'm not sure how much longer we can go without a serious meltdown."

"What do we do?"

"We've got to decide where we go from here."

"What are our options?"

"You could turn yourself in with Adam. He'd get stabilized quickly."

"With what?" She heard the horror in her own voice. "Foster care?"

Harlan nodded.

"You know as well as I do that's not a viable option for him. He needs us. He needs both of us." The words and the intimacy they implied surprised her, but she knew they were true. "We're all he's got now." The words struck deeply and something inside her trembled when she said them. She knew what it was like not to have a support system. She wouldn't let that happen to Adam.

"Yes, but if we get ourselves arrested or worse, can you imagine what that will be like for him?"

"No, I can't." Gina squeezed her eyes shut. "Strangers taking care of him…that's…" She couldn't think about it at all; it was too much.

Harlan gave her hand a slight squeeze. His grip was warm, reassuring. Tempted to lean into that comfort, she longed to forget about this hideous, heinous day and melt into the blanketing embrace of his arms. What would that be like? To completely lose herself in him. She knew he could blot out the horror, even if only for a couple of hours.

"We don't have to figure this out tonight." Harlan's voice jerked her back to the now.

Why was she thinking like this? Sarah was dead and instead of grieving for her, Gina was imagining what it would be like to sink into sexual oblivion with this man. Was she going completely mad?

Harlan continued, seemingly unaware Gina was on a schizophrenic roller coaster of emotion. "You need to rest. I made up a bed in the other room for you. Why don't you get cleaned up and get some sleep. We'll talk more in the morning."

Gina opened her eyes and tried to put on a game face. So tired of feeling vulnerable and emotionally ragged. This latest had her worried she was losing her mind. And she hated the out-of-control helplessness. "All right, that sounds like a good idea."

She started to sit up when Harlan pointed toward the phone in her lap. "Who was that?" he asked cautiously.

"Clay, my boss. Rather, my former boss." *How long had Harlan stood there listening?* "Obviously we had a...closer relationship. A long time ago."

She felt herself blushing again and huffed a rueful laugh. "There's nothing funny about what he said, but I guess I'd better take my comic relief where I can get it today. Even if it's laughing at what a fool I was."

Harlan didn't respond, he just fixed those gray eyes on her and she kept talking, hoping she wasn't babbling. "He fired Tammy this afternoon, and then he caught her trying to smuggle the envelope out of the office to me. He said he gave it to the FBI."

"Damn."

"We're screwed, aren't we?"

"I don't know. Do you think he was telling the truth?"

"Not sure. He was drunk. He said he fired the whole creative team at closing. That would have been at the same time we were there to pick up the package."

Harlan was still staring and she heard herself begin to prattle. *What was he thinking behind that inscrutable gaze?* She had no idea and it unnerved her. *Was he mad, sad, bored, turned on?* Mentally she shook herself. No, there was no way it could be the latter. She was the only one entertaining that particular fantasy.

"So it's no wonder Tammy hasn't called. She's probably furious with me. If she wasn't going to call the police, she probably wishes she had now."

"You think she'll hold it against you?" he asked.

"Well, not forever, but long enough to go out and have a few drinks with the other folks who got fired on my account. I can't say as I blame her."

"So at best she would need the evening to cool off before you talk to her."

"Or sober up, yeah… I guarantee they're drowning their sorrows with martinis and margaritas at Gloria's."

"So, we wait till the morning to contact her."

She glanced at her watch. It was just after 1:00 a.m. "Yes, definitely later in the morning." She rose from the easy chair, her bones feeling as ancient as the creaky recliner sounded. "I'll go get cleaned up." She wrinkled her nose. Her shirt smelled faintly of urine. Could Harlan smell it, too?

"Put your clothes outside the bathroom door, and I'll run a load of laundry," he offered.

Well, that certainly solidified the answer to her earlier question. Urine-scented clothing was not high on anyone's list of turn-ons. "Thanks, these jeans could walk themselves to the machine."

He smiled faintly. "Just try and get some sleep, Gina. We can't do anything tonight."

"You're right. There's nothing we can do." *Except worry about what happens tomorrow.*

Chapter Ten

Harlan stood on the deck and studied the night sky. Behind him he heard the bathwater running and thought about Gina undressing in the same small steamy room he'd been standing in a few minutes ago. He tried to imagine what it would be like to be here with her under different circumstances, when she wasn't swimming in grief in that antique bathtub the size of a small pool.

What would it be like to be here without every cop and his dog looking for them? Cool air blew against his face, and the curtains billowed back into the living room behind him. He gazed at the stars, wondering how in hell things had become such a mess in less than a week.

Four nights ago he'd been waiting for Sarah to get home from work, thinking about the class assignment he was working on and playing trains with Adam on the floor in her den. Then the world changed, with one phone call. The hell of it was, he'd made the call.

Jordan Bell had answered on the third ring, glad to hear from him and not at all concerned about the lateness of the hour. "Harlan, is everything all right?"

"No, it's not. Sarah Sutton's disappeared and the police aren't paying any attention. I need your help. I've got her sister on the way from Dallas to get the little boy, but no one here seems to give a damn that she's gone."

There was a long silence, and a prickling sensation raised hairs on the back of his neck. "Are you hearing me?"

Finally Jordan answered. "I was worried something might happen." He sounded old and weary, and it wasn't just the static over the phone line.

"What's going on?"

"Harlan, I need you to stay with the boy until I figure this out."

"What are you talking about?"

"I don't know. Honestly, I don't. But I was worried this was where things were headed. You need to keep an eye on that boy."

"J.B., I'm through taking orders—you know that." Harlan didn't hide the warning in his own voice. "I need more information."

"I can't give it to you…I can only say she was doing some work for me. I didn't think it was dangerous, but apparently some people were upset about it."

"What? What people?"

"People I owe, Harlan. People who helped me get here. You're familiar with that, aren't you?" There was a dark tone to the question as the arrow hit home.

"Why didn't you tell me this when I came down here?"

"Because you were looking for something to soothe your conscience about…things. I gave it you. Sarah Sutton truly needed help. You provided it. I needed someone there on site. You provided that as well."

Harlan was stunned and temporarily speechless. That the man he'd thought of as a father would use him in such a way. J.B. had sent him here purposely, when Harlan had thought he was coming home simply to heal. His anger bubbled to the surface when the greater implications became clear. "Why didn't you tell me to keep an eye on Sarah if you knew she was in danger?"

"I didn't know she was in any real danger. At worst, I thought her house or lab might get broken into. Never anything like this."

There was another long, uncomfortable silence. Harlan couldn't believe he'd been used like this…again.

J.B. tried another tack, his voice calm and reasonable. "I don't even know if that's what's happened. But I need you to keep an eye on things. Take care of that boy. Save someone you can."

Jordan's words echoed in his mind. So much like Jimmy's as he lay dying on that road in Iraq. The older man's voice brought him back to the conversation at hand. "So we're set? You'll take care of the boy?"

Harlan didn't hesitate. "Of course."

"Good. I'll see if I can find out anything from the police about Sarah and get more information. Call me when the sister gets there or if you hear anything."

"Right."

Harlan snapped his phone shut, cursing under his breath. He was being played. He knew it and Jordan knew it. But with Adam in the mix, Harlan was powerless to tell the man to screw himself. He was stuck.

Harlan wasn't doing a damn thing except taking care of the boy until he knew more. He couldn't believe he'd been put in this position. J.B. knew how he felt about being put in positions where he couldn't say no. Especially now.

Jesus. Jordan had been the only one Harlan had talked to when he'd gotten home after Jimmy died. Why hadn't he told Harlan that Sarah was in danger?

His mentor, his best friend's father. Jordan had always assured Harlan that he didn't blame him for Jimmy's death. But still… The unpleasant thought raced across Harlan's mind before he could check it. Perhaps Jordan hadn't told Harlan about Sarah's being in danger because he knew Harlan would blame himself, or maybe J.B. had planned all this from the very beginning.

Standing on Sarah's lake house deck less than a week later, he was still shaking his head. A voice asking a favor. Asking for help. Harlan owed him and there'd been nothing to say but *yes*. So he'd stayed with Adam and Gina. If he'd known then what he knew now, would he have done this any differently?

He wasn't sure. But not having a choice in the matter made him edgy. Feeling obligated made him angry. And now he suspected he was being set up. Feeling guilty about Jimmy's death made everything worse. Wondering if he could have done anything to save Kate Brooks or Sarah Sutton would haunt him for the rest of his life.

JORDAN BELL HANDED his coat to the junior staffer. It had been a long day, but the session had gone as expected. The hearings would be over early next week.

There had been no real surprises and for that he was grateful. He couldn't stand any more surprises. The recommendations of the committee for a liability waiver would stand as they'd been written a month before.

He nodded to the group before him. "Good evening, Senator."

At the door his administrative assistant stopped him. "There's a call for you, sir. Line two from Kentucky. Are you in?"

He took a deep breath. "Yes, Valerie." *I'm always in for Marnie.* He strode into his inner sanctum, sank into the leather seat and scooped up the receiver.

"You've had a predictable day, Jordan," cooed the disembodied voice.

"Yes, I have."

"No unexpected news or unsettling conclusions from the studies?"

"None at all. The recommendations were all as we expected."

"Since PharmaVax is paying the bills, that's not a surprise." A harsh laugh rolled out of the phone. It was not a pleasant sound. "What about that other matter?"

"The university study from Mississippi never materialized." *You made damn sure of that, didn't you.*

The woman's voice was scoffing. "Apparently all talk."

"Hmm. That's the case sometimes," said Jordan.

"Too bad." The PharmaVax employee... contractor—whatever the hell she called herself, almost sounded bored.

"For whom?" Jordan had already discovered earlier this week that arguing was useless. He felt the first crushing band of pain around his chest.

"Certainly not PharmaVax."

"Yes," he answered through clenched teeth and inhaled deeply. *But the girl?*

"When will the recommendations go to the floor for a vote?"

"The liability waiver for the Indonesian flu vaccine is attached to a bill on the fast track. It should be there Sunday afternoon."

"Excellent."

"So our agreement still holds?" He heard his own voice shake and looked longingly at the credenza beside him. The cut crystal decanter of scotch. He hadn't needed a drink this desperately in a long time, since Jimmy died.

"Absolutely. The funds will be there."

"Fine."

"Remember, we have over thirty of these in the pipeline. It will be quite lucrative for you."

The pain struck at his solar plexus. *Thirty? Judas Priest.* He couldn't imagine getting through this one. "Right."

He hung up the phone and took another deep breath, feeling as if he'd just run a marathon and made a deal with the devil to finish the race. He exhaled and rolled the chair sideways to pour a generous glass of Glenlivet. He tossed back two drinks before his hands stopped trembling.

For the first time since he'd embarked on this journey, he was truly frightened. Not like he was with the chest pains from the panic attacks, but concerned for his life and that of people he'd once cared for. There was more at stake here than he'd ever dreamed of at the beginning. Would he have agreed if he'd known what would be required before it was all over?

He took another sip of the liquor and felt a soothing warmth begin to steal over him. Two more days, three at the most, and his part was over.

For now.

He took another deep breath and finished his scotch. He could do it. He had to. The reward was irresistible. Even if the entity he was dealing with made Satan look tame.

Chapter Eleven

Gina woke to the sun streaming into the window of the cabin's master bedroom. Half the furniture was shrouded in sheets, and dust motes danced in the light. Her head felt as if it were stuffed with cotton; then everything from yesterday came rushing back.

Sarah was dead.

Gina wanted nothing more than to stay right where she was. She covered her face with the slightly musty-smelling bedspread and closed her eyes, wishing for the oblivion of sleep. Her cell phone trilled the calypso tune that had sounded so cheerful when she chose it but now seemed obscenely obnoxious.

With her head still covered, she reached out, knocking something to the floor as she fumbled to answer. "Hello?"

"Gina, it's Tammy. Are you okay? You awake?"

Gina shook her head to clear the last of the cobwebs and sorrow.

"I'm hanging in there," she managed.

"I saw the news…about Sarah. I can't believe this happened. I'm so sorry, honey. Are you safe?"

Gina looked around again at the bedroom and wondered how long it would take the police to figure out the corporate ownership for the cabin. "For a while, I think."

"Is the man you're with responsible for this?"

"God, no. I was with him at that house the day before yesterday. Sarah wasn't there. We left two days ago. Whoever killed Sarah did it after we left and set things up to make it look like Harlan was guilty. I've been with him the whole time."

Except when he went to Wal-Mart and Adam had his meltdown. But there hadn't been time for Harlan to go home and come back. She pushed the niggle of doubt aside to examine later.

"It's a setup, Tammy, I swear it."

"Okay." Tammy sounded doubtful.

"I spoke to Clay." Changing the subject seemed vital at this point. "He told me he fired you and the whole team. I can't believe he did that."

"He called a mandatory emergency meeting right after we talked. I couldn't even call you back. That horse's ass fired us all on the spot. That's why I didn't meet you downstairs."

"He told me. Tammy, I'm sorry."

"Why? Because Clay's a raving lunatic and his wife's a bitch?"

Gina smiled sadly. "No, because I can't help but feel responsible for this."

"Don't. Besides, I've got the papers Sarah sent."

"What? How?" Gina sat up in bed, not quite believing this could be true. "Clay said he'd turned them over to the FBI."

"Oh, that." Gina could see Tammy waving her hands as she talked, just as if they were sitting in their cubicle at Dixon Meyers. "I opened the FedEx after we talked and put Sarah's papers in my purse."

"So what did the FBI get?"

"They got the proofs for the King Dog Food campaign. I was out of envelopes and put the photos of that prizewinning Great Dane in Sarah's FedEx for our meeting. Clay never looked inside the envelope after security took it out of my briefcase. The dumbass fired me before I could tell him what was really in there."

"Oh my God. That's perfect."

Tammy hooted. "It gets better. Those proofs were due last

night to the client. Clay is probably having a seizure about now. Is revenge sweet or what?"

Gina laughed out loud and felt traitorous tears begin to well at the corners of her eyes. She scrubbed them away with the back of her hand. She longed to lean her head back and gab like they used to at work. Just spill it all.

But Tammy had already paid enough for being her friend. And she had Sarah's papers. "Where can I meet you to get the package?" asked Gina.

"I can come to you."

"You don't have to do that. You've done enough. We'll come get it."

"All right. But I'm actually leaving in a little while. You know where the key is. I'll put the papers on the kitchen table in case I miss you. Where are you now?"

"We're in—"

"Gina?" Harlan was standing in the doorway. In a pair of sweatpants and nothing else.

Her eyes lingered on his rippled chest and flat stomach for a moment before she felt herself blush. She had no idea how long he'd been standing there listening, and now she'd been caught staring at his half-naked body. She covered the mouthpiece and forced herself to focus on his unshaven face.

"What?" she asked irritably.

"Don't tell her where we are," he almost whispered the words.

How had he known? She frowned at him, even as she realized he was right and tried not to be distracted by his state of undress again.

"We're at a hotel near Sherman," she said, starting to pull the sheet over her bare legs. The lie slipped off her tongue far easier than she would have liked.

"Well, if you need a place, you're welcome to stay here," Tammy offered.

Gina felt the guilt creeping over her, followed by another blush to the tips of her toes. She squeezed her eyes shut against the onslaught of emotion. "Tammy, do you know what you're asking for? You've seen the news. We're wanted by everyone but your Aunt Bessie right now. And I'm— God, I'm a wreck."

This was such an about-face from yesterday. Gina tried not to let Tammy's change of attitude throw her. She hated that she wasn't sure if it was sympathy for Sarah or a setup.

Tammy's voice brought her back to the present. "I'm not going to turn you away. After this crap yesterday, screw the system. Come to my house. I'm not even going to be here tonight. Jack has tickets to hear Diamond Rio in Fort Worth. We're spending the night. It's not like I've got to be at work on Monday."

Tammy laughed sadly. "I'm leaving Martin, the wonder dog, in the backyard. Key's in the flowerpot. Help yourself to whatever is in the fridge, and feel free to use the shower." She sounded anxious to help.

"Thanks. I really appreciate it. I'm not sure what we're going to do right now. Can I call you back?"

"Sure, but you don't even have to let me know. If you're here before I leave, great. If not, that's all right, too. Stay if you want. Don't stay. Whatever works."

"Tammy, thank you. After everything…" *This has cost you.* Gina didn't have to say it.

"You hang in there, girl. It's going to be okay."

"You, too." Gina nodded and shut the phone, momentarily overwhelmed by her friend's kindness.

When she looked up, Harlan was still leaning in her doorway—seemingly oblivious to how distracting his bicep muscles and six-pack abs might be to any woman with a pulse. Gina was suddenly aware that she had slept in only a T-shirt, but this news couldn't wait.

"Tammy has the papers, and she says we can stay at her apartment." Using her foot, she tried to unobtrusively pull more covers over her legs. After two false starts she gave up trying to be non-chalant and reached down to pull the blanket and sheet to her waist.

"Do you trust her?"

She'd expected him to ask that. "I don't know." She shrugged. "I think so. She's not going to be there tonight, and she's going to Fort Worth for the day. We'd have the place to ourselves."

He looked around at the covered furniture in the bedroom and her newly arranged bedclothes. His eyes were indecipherable.

"How long before you think they'll figure out we're here?" she asked.

He shook his head. "I've no idea. It's a gamble, a risk, either way. But the longer we stay in one place…" His words trailed off.

"The bigger the risk of someone finding us."

He nodded.

"I didn't tell her yes or no. And she didn't care. I don't see how that could be a trap, unless they're watching just in case we show. I think she would have pressed me if she was trying to set us up."

He nodded. "You're right. And we've got to get a look at those papers. Since you said she's going to leave them for us and we can stop by anytime, let's figure out where we're going once we have Sarah's package."

Gina spoke without hesitation. "To Washington."

"Washington?" That pronouncement had him leaving his spot in the doorway and coming to stand at the foot of her bed.

"I need to get them to Senator Bell like Sarah asked. More now than ever."

"You think you can just waltz in there to see him with our faces all over the news?"

She sighed. "I haven't gotten that far yet. But he is a Mississippi senator, and Sarah was a constituent of his. Can't you go to see your senator?"

"As long as you aren't wanted by the police in several states, I'm sure you can. What about Adam?"

"What about him?" asked Gina.

"Is he going with us?"

Gina sighed again. "Of course. Where is he now?"

Harlan jerked his head toward the den.

"I don't hear him."

"He's not talking."

"Oh." Gina's own voice was subdued.

"He can't do it. We can't drag him across the country like this. A road trip to Washington will be extraordinarily difficult." Harlan gripped the footboard and leaned forward. "He can't handle much more of this kind of disruption. He needs stability, predictability. You should consider calling the cops before this goes any further."

She shook her head. "Nothing's changed, not as far as what will happen to Adam if I call the police. I understand he needs peace, but don't you see? Unless we figure this out, his life is going to be nothing but chaos for the foreseeable future. If I give up, I'm giving him up as well, and that's not something I'll even consider."

She straightened against the headboard and leaned forward. "Once Sarah's documentation is in the right hands, there's no reason for anyone to come after us anymore. The cat's out of the bag, so to speak, and we're free of this."

"You hope." He stared at her for a long moment with those intense gray eyes. Again she had no idea what he was thinking. He straightened and turned toward the hallway without a word.

"Wait," she called. "Are you going to help me?"

He turned back. "Help you do what?"

"Help me get those papers to Senator Bell."

He stared at her again. Silence hung in the air. No matter what, she wasn't going to be the first to break the eye contact. She stared without blinking, the air charged with something she couldn't or wouldn't define.

Finally he looked away. "Well, are you getting up, or what? We've got a lot to do today."

Without waiting for a reply, he sauntered down the hall, the sweatpants riding low on his hips. Gina sat there, caught up in contemplating their exchange and his retreating back. The muscles there were as well-defined as his six-pack abs had been.

She didn't want to know why he'd capitulated. Harlan didn't strike her as a man who gave in easily, and she wasn't about to question his motivation when his help was so desperately needed. Nor was she going to reflect on that electricity in the air when he was with her. She had enough on her plate.

Especially now.

GINA SLID OUT of the passenger seat and hurried to Tammy's first-floor apartment door while Harlan stayed with Adam in the car. When Tammy didn't answer her knock, Gina assumed she was in the shower or otherwise indisposed and pulled out her cell phone.

When there was no answer, she headed around the side of the building to Tammy's private fenced-in patio-and-yard area. The gate was unlocked and opened noiselessly.

The curtains on the sliding door were drawn. She rapped on the equally darkened window and waited impatiently in front of the slider, preparing to dig around for the spare key under Tammy's copper flowerpot. The wind was picking up, and the temperature had dropped. Goose bumps rose on her arms.

Where was Martin?

By now the faithful but sometimes misguided watchdog should have been raising the roof. There was no sound from inside, no loud television or music playing. Not one tiny yip. Nothing that would have kept Tammy from hearing her knock or the phone ring. Gina tried the door.

It, too opened soundlessly. The curtains billowed back into the room as a gust of wind blew steadily stronger behind her.

Papers blew off the coffee table and littered the floor of the tiny living room. Tammy was nowhere to be seen.

A manila envelope peeked out from behind one of the sofa cushions. On impulse Gina reached over and pulled it out. Tammy's familiar handwriting was scrawled across the front. *Gina Rodgers.*

Then she heard it.

Whining and scratching coming from the back.

"Martin?" she called, walking toward the two bedrooms in back.

More whining. Then frantic barking.

She opened the hall closet door, and Martin, all twelve pounds of him, exploded into her arms, barking, jumping, licking, crying.

"What is it, boy? What's going on?" Tucking the envelope under her arm, she scooped up the wriggling puppy and patted the wiry fur on the dachshund terrier mix as she wandered back toward the kitchen. "How did you get locked in there? Tammy would never put you in— Oh, God."

Gina stopped in the middle of the living room when she saw her. Tammy. On the tile floor. Lying in a puddle of—

No, oh, God, no. Not blood.

Her shirt was soaked red with it. The yellow blouse they'd bought together a month ago at a Nordstrom sale.

Tammy's vacant eyes stared sightlessly at the ceiling.

This couldn't be happening.

Her throat had been cut almost to the bone.

Gina was staring at the wound when she realized the coppery scent of blood permeated the room. How had she missed that smell when she'd opened the door earlier?

She had to get out. Now. Bile rose in the back of Gina's throat. Martin yipped, frantic to get out of her arms.

She backed toward the glass sliding door, clutching the dog to her belly, only to get tangled in the billowing curtains. Desperately clawing at the fabric with one hand and holding Martin in the other, she stumbled across the threshold into Harlan's chest.

"Move, move." She pushed the hysterical dog into his arms, dashed to the edge of the patio and made it past the shrubbery just as her stomach revolted, retching until she wept. When she was done, Harlan handed her a wet washcloth. She plopped down on the small patch of concrete, her legs no longer able to support her.

"Where's Martin?" A ridiculous question under the circumstances.

Harlan nodded to the yard, where Adam was holding the small dog and Dickens together in his arms and smiling for the first time in almost twenty-four hours. Martin was licking the child's face and wagging his tail in ecstasy while the child patted his head and back, laughing with true abandon.

Gina squeezed her eyes shut, trying to process everything that had just happened. The vision of Tammy lying on the kitchen floor in the blood-soaked shirt was so vivid that her eyes popped back open to watch Adam instead.

She shook her head and swallowed hard. Hot tears scalded her face as the breeze continued to blow the curtains into the living room.

Everything was just as it had been moments before, only everything had changed…again.

"Who would do that? Why would they do that?" she asked. Harlan sat beside her.

"I don't know. It looks like it happened right before we got here. This wasn't random, Gina."

"She died because of us, didn't she?"

He didn't answer.

"We've got to call the police, don't we?"

"Yes, but I'd suggest we do it after we leave here."

There was a long beat of silence.

"Oh my God, we'll be suspects here, too, won't we?" She looked at the envelope in her hands and lifted the opened flap with shaking fingers.

Inside were papers but not from her sister. They were invoices from Dixon Meyers. It took a moment before Gina realized what they were. Requisitions signed by her for various items they'd used at photo shoots.

Designer bags, clothing, designer shoes—window dressing items—all legitimate and authorized by Clay and the customer. But put together in this format, it appeared she'd been pilfering from the company. Not necessarily a motive for murder, but certainly enough to tarnish her credibility. She remembered pulling the package from under the sofa cushion, where investigators had been meant to find it. No doubt there was other damning evidence inside as well.

Harlan nodded. "Whoever's pulling the strings here has made sure of that."

"We need to leave now, don't we?"

"We needed to leave ten minutes ago." He stood and offered his hand.

She still tasted the bile in her mouth, only now it was spiked with a metallic taste of fear. She looked around at the small patio area. Adam was lying on his back in the grass with Martin jumping over his belly.

Later she would be grateful for the dramatic change the dog had wrought and the way the two had fallen in love with each other. For now she and Harlan scooped up the boy and the dog and hurried toward the car. They were coming through the gate that faced the neighbor's small patio when a huge bald man opened his sliding glass door.

"Hey!" shouted the surprised man.

"Move it, and don't look directly at him," murmured Harlan, pulling his baseball cap lower.

"Hey, stop," yelled the neighbor again.

Harlan grabbed her arm.

"Run."

Chapter Twelve

Harlan picked up Adam with one arm and pulled Gina along with the other. They scrambled into the car and sped out of the parking slot as the portly neighbor came barreling out his front door.

"You think he saw our plates?" Gina looked out the back window.

"I don't know." Harlan fishtailed out of the lot and took a right into traffic, punching the accelerator. "We may need to change them again or do something. Give me a minute."

Gina turned around and stared out the windshield, still struggling to process everything that had just happened. Tammy was dead. God, she couldn't even think about that right now. Not on top of Sarah's death.

Gina was apparently being set up. Sarah's study was well and truly gone. Why was this happening? Who would be doing this?

The same people who had hurt Sarah? Why? What did they have to gain now?

Martin yapped, and Gina glanced into the back, where the dog and boy continued to bond. Adam jabbered away delightedly at the puppy. Martin seemed particularly fascinated with Dickens. Adam lifted the stuffed dino over his head.

"No bite Dickens," he commanded.

Martin sat down on the seat.

Everything seemed to come back to the information from Kate Brooks. Could the pharmaceutical companies be that serious about not letting Sarah's study come to light? It was going to happen anyway when the study was published by the tuna company. So why did it matter? Gina and Harlan didn't even have the information. And with Tammy's death, it now appeared they never would. Why would anyone be after them?

"No, doggy, no."

The love affair was obviously cooling. Adam's little voice rose to a shrill pitch.

Gina turned to see Adam and Martin engaged in a tug-of-war over the stuffed animal. Gina saw it happening in slow motion but could do nothing to stop the inevitable.

"No!" Adam shrieked as the head ripped off the dinosaur. "No!"

Martin dropped the dinosaur head and scurried under the seat as Adam dissolved into what Gina suspected would be inconsolable tears.

Harlan adjusted the rearview mirror. "Oh, crap," he mumbled under his breath. Gina climbed over the console to survey the damage as he pulled into a convenience store parking lot.

"Dead!" shrieked Adam. "Dead!"

She slipped an arm around Adam's shoulders to give him a squeeze, but he wriggled out from under her touch and moved toward the door. She longed to hold him and wipe those tears but focused instead on what she hoped would bring the greatest relief.

She lifted the dinosaur head from the floorboard where Martin had dropped it. Bits of stuffing drifted out of the bottom of neck. The dog huddled under the backseat, peering anxiously out from under the seat belt anchor, quite cognizant of the fact that he was in deep trouble.

Gina shot Martin a dirty look. She wasn't feeling very forgiving right now. Apparently Adam wasn't, either.

The boy clutched the decapitated dino body in both hands.

"Dead," he cried as tears poured down his cheeks. "Bad dog!" He glared at Martin.

"Can I see him?" Gina asked softly. The situation didn't look completely hopeless. She wasn't an award-winning seamstress, but she'd had a roommate in college working on a degree in fashion design. She knew more than most about sewing a hem or straight seam.

Adam held up Dickens's battered body and sniffed loudly.

"May I hold him?" she asked.

At first, Adam didn't want to let her, but he finally relented. Some of the fluff stuck to his sticky hands as the dino body landed with a plop in her palm. She put the two pieces together. Dickens's well-loved status had apparently loosened the original neck seams, Martin's tug-of-war game had done the rest.

"I can fix this." She leaned forward from the backseat to show Harlan. "Not good as new, but I can reattach the head."

"Even with as big a hurry as we're in, I think you'd better do it now." Harlan watched Adam as he sat with big tears streaming down his face.

"I need a needle and thread."

Harlan reached back and wiped Adam's face with the cuff of his denim shirt. "Right." He exited the car for the convenience store.

Adam began rocking as Gina searched the floorboard for any other stuffing that might have fallen out. She found a half-dollar-size chunk of batting and was shoving it in when she felt a hard edge inside the lower part of the dinosaur.

She turned away from Adam so he wouldn't see her gutting his beloved stuffed animal and shoved her finger in the neck. Her fingertip touched something solid.

She looked at the belly of the dinosaur and noticed that the stitching there was different, the thread a slightly different color. Had something been put inside him? Rising excitement combined with a sense of dread. She glanced over her shoulder at Adam, who was staring out the window.

Not wanting him to see what she was about to do, she climbed back over the front seat. Turning Dickens over on his tummy, she tried to loosen the threads from the neck down. They ripped with a sickening sound. She glanced at Adam to see if he'd heard. He was still gazing at the parking lot.

Reminding herself that she had to be able to sew Dickens back together after dissecting him, she dug in her purse for a pen. Sliding the pointed edge of the lid underneath the loosened threads, she opened the animal down the back. Martin whined as she worked. She spared a moment to pat him on the head, her uncharitable feelings toward him from earlier forgiven.

She'd gotten three stitches out when Harlan opened the door and sat down. "Hey, I thought the point was to put it back togeth—"

He stopped talking as she pulled back the brown plush material to reveal a computer thumb drive memory stick surrounded by cotton batting.

Gina nodded as her hands stilled. "Sarah, always hiding things in plain sight."

He reached over to pull the memory stick from the batting. "What do you think? The study?"

She stared at the flash drive and thought of Sarah's voice mail from two days earlier. *As long as you keep Dickens close, he's happy.* "Oh, yeah. I'm sure of it."

She leaned toward him and pulled the cover off the tip of the drive. "Final report with M.D.," she murmured under her breath. "Mr. Dickens."

"You think this is what everyone is after?"

"Absolutely." She stopped for a moment. "Having this changes everything."

Sarah's voice still echoed in her head. *Take care of him for me, okay?* "Once the study is out in the open, there's no reason for 'them' to come after us anymore, right? I mean, the cat's out of the bag then. Why bother?"

"A lot of 'ifs' there. First we need to find out for sure what's on the stick. Meanwhile here's everything you need to repair

Dickens." Harlan handed her a small bag emblazoned with the convenience store logo. "I hope, anyway. I didn't know you'd be performing major surgery here."

A small voice from the backseat caught their attention. "Dickens dead, Mommy dead."

They both looked over their shoulders at Adam. He rocked on the seat, occasionally mumbling.

"Jesus," Harlan muttered.

Gina shook her head. "He won't let me near him. But once I have Dickens back together, I think he'll be better." She reshaped the dinosaur's tummy with her fingers.

Harlan started the engine. "How's the dog?"

Reaching under the seat, she patted Martin's nose. "Still cowering. He doesn't handle rejection well."

"Does any man?"

She rolled her eyes and dumped the supplies in her lap. "Where are we going?"

She held up the thread, and Harlan gave an apologetic shrug. Fluorescent-green. Not exactly a dead-on match. Hopefully Adam wouldn't mind Dickens having a new accent stripe to mark his brush with death.

"An airstrip in Addison, about twenty minutes away. A friend is going to meet us there."

"What?" Gina almost dropped the needle she was threading.

"A buddy of mine with a private plane is going to fly us out of here."

"Oh." She was at a loss for more to say and began sewing the dinosaur back together instead.

One stitch up. One stitch down. Slow and steady, like breathing. Sewing Dickens together was the first normal thing she'd done in four days.

"I think that's the only thing to do," continued Harlan. "Too many people are looking for us. I'm not sure if Tammy's neighbor got the license number on this car, but we know he's probably calling the police and giving our description to them.

"Then there's whoever did that to Tammy. Somehow they knew you were going to see her and they set you up. There's nowhere left in town for us to go, and driving this vehicle won't be an option much longer."

Tammy.

Gina was horrified to realize that in the few moments she'd been dealing with the "Dickens crisis," she'd let herself forget about Tammy and the bloodbath in her home. That must make her a horrible friend, in addition to being a horrible sister.

"It doesn't, you know."

She was staring out the windshield when Harlan's words sunk in.

"What?" She didn't turn from looking at the road.

"It doesn't make you a bad person because you forgot for a while."

She turned, but he wasn't looking at her. He was focused on the road. "How did you—"

"Know what you were thinking?" He stopped at a light and pinned her with those gray eyes.

She nodded slowly.

"It's called surviving, Gina. Remember? That's what this is about right now. The grieving for your friend, for your sister. You'll do that later. Right now, it's all about getting through this. Just put one foot in front of the other until you get to a safe place."

"But where is a safe place?" she murmured.

"That's pretty relative right now, isn't it?" He refocused on the road. "My friend is meeting us at the Addison Airport in a couple of hours. We can park and wait there and then get on the plane with no one ever seeing us."

She started sewing again. One stitch up. One stitch down. Breathe in. Breathe out. She found she couldn't talk anymore, just listen.

"Since we've got a couple of hours, I'd like to find out what's on that memory stick. You okay with that?" He drove with one hand on the steering wheel and his other arm stretched along the back of the seat between them. His fingertips almost brushed the top of her shoulder.

She nodded slowly. One stitch up. One stitch down.

"We need an Internet café or something like it." Harlan was talking more to himself than to her, but apparently he noticed when she didn't reply.

"Gina?"

"What?" Her voice sounded brittle even to her own ears.

"Are you okay?"

She sighed. "I don't know. This is all happening so fast." She found she couldn't look at him as she finished the dinosaur's back and began reattaching the head. "Where will we go?"

He stopped at another light. "There's a Kinko's. Perfect."

"I meant where are we flying to? And who is this friend?" She put her hand on his arm and stared at him now, her reticence to make eye contact forgotten.

"A military buddy who owes me a favor. He's a pilot who made good in the private sector. I told him we needed to get to Washington. I think that's the best place to be with this information—" he held up the flash drive "—*if* this is your sister's study."

He stared back until the light turned and someone behind them honked. In the back parking lot of Kinko's, they agreed it would be easier for him to go into the store alone while Gina and Adam waited in the car.

"If I'm gone longer than ten minutes, you leave and go to the Addison Airport. Where's your pen?"

"I don't understand," Gina protested, even as she dug in her bag and jotted the number Harlan recited on the fleshy part of her palm.

"Gina, someone might recognize me. Our pictures have been plastered all over the newspapers and television, even out here. Texas is a concealed carry state, remember?"

"Then why don't we just wait?"

"Because I think what's on this memory stick is pretty damned important. Come on, usually these folks pay little or no attention to their customers' faces, only their wallets. This is just a precaution. It's going to be fine."

"But—" she began.

"If I'm not back in ten minutes, I'm not coming back. You and Adam get out of here. Understand? Call Shaun Logan at that number." He pointed at her hand. "He'll tell you what to do."

She looked at the back of the store. From this vantage point it looked harmless enough, but if something happened to Harlan... The thought of Gina being on her own with Adam in this situation made her stomach cramp. The thought of something happening to Harlan made her stomach roil.

"Look at the clock now, Gina."

She did.

"It's 12:07. At 12:17 you leave. Got it?"

She nodded, reluctantly.

"Okay." He moved to get out of the car.

"Wait." She grabbed his arm with one hand and dug in her purse again for the Kinko's copy card she had from work. She couldn't quite believe she'd remembered it. "I don't know how much is left on this, but you should be able to bypass the self-service kiosk inside."

"Thanks." He gave her the smile that had taken her breath away the first night she met him, then handed her the keys and reached back to pat Adam on the head. "See ya later, buddy. 12:17, Gina."

"Yes, I know."

"Good." He started to get out again and then leaned back in, and before she knew what he intended, he was kissing her. A "see you soon" kind of kiss. Full of promise and expectation. Before she could respond he smiled at her and got out.

"12:17," he mouthed through the window.

Shaken, Gina looked down at the stuffed animal in her lap and resumed sewing. He'd probably done that to piss her off so she wouldn't think about being scared. It had worked, or at least she wasn't scared anymore.

Stitch up, stitch down.

She liked the kiss better than his snarky comments when they'd been parked downtown outside the ad agency.

Breathe in. Breathe out.

How had she ever thought anything about this felt normal?

Chapter Thirteen

Harlan walked through the glass sliding doors to the sound of Muzak. A clerk with multicolored hair barely glanced up from working on a large printer. Security cameras mounted behind the counter gave a view of the entire store.

He decided to ignore the cameras, since there was no getting away from them, and headed straight to the business center in the back. He didn't plan to be here long enough for security to be an issue. To the right of the computer area was a restroom. A man in business attire worked at one of the small cubicles.

Harlan sat at the computer closest to the fire exit with his back to the wall. He slid Gina's copy card into the debit reader and was grateful to see she had thirty dollars credit.

He pressed the flash drive into the USB port and waited for the screen to come up as he looked around the store. The businessman still typed away three cubes down from him, and the clerk worked on a different machine behind the counter while talking on a cell phone.

The flash drive opened, and a menu popped up. Only two items. The first was titled Study. The second, Letter. He hit Study and read the initial paragraph.

This was it. Sarah's research—*The Effects of Organic and Ethyl Mercury on the Developing Brains of Chimpanzees.*

He scrolled through the document. Thirty pages of graphs, charts and information that seemed fairly incomprehensible until the last page.

Surprisingly the control groups yielded the most information. The data from these groups prove definitively that ethyl mercury, otherwise known as thimerosal, does indeed cause significant neurological damage to the developing brain. A logical conclusion follows that injecting thimerosal into the bodies of babies with developing brains would be harmful and detrimental.

Yes, that would be exactly what Kate Brooks had told them. A death knell for the vaccine manufacturers. He hit Print for the entire document and went back to the menu on the flash drive to see that second item. He opened the file titled Letter, and his heart broke.

Dearest Adam,
The day you read this we'll both know you've grown up and I wasn't there to see it. I want to tell you how proud I am of you and how much I love you. Your aunt Gina loves you, too.
   I so wanted to be there—

He stopped, unwilling to read any more, feeling as if he were intruding. Instead he hit Print. Sarah must have known something was going to happen if she wrote this.

His phone rang. Gina's number. "Yeah?"

"Harlan, the police are here."

"What?" He looked out the window but saw nothing.

"They're around the corner by me. Two cars. They drove in with lights and no sirens. I don't think they have the plates on this car, but they're watching the building. They met a clerk with extreme hair by the Dumpster."

"Damn." Harlan looked at the computer on the desk in front of him. Staring hard at the card in the debit reader, he felt like an idiot. "Gina, did you buy this copy card with a credit card or cash?"

There was a long silence.

"Oh my God. I'm so sorry. It was the company card but in my name. You think they traced it that fast?"

Yep. Harlan gave a noncommittal sound and slowly scanned the counter area, now mindful of the cameras he'd seen on the way in. The clerk was nowhere to be seen. The businessman was still sitting at the cubicle, oblivious.

Harlan thought through his options. Security cameras staged above the counter meant he could be seen from where he was sitting right now, if someone was watching. And more than likely, someone was. He leaned back for a moment and stared at the ceiling—the suspended type with tiles.

Gina's voice sounded soft in his ear. "Two officers are going around the front. The other two are still out back. One of them is walking toward the fire exit."

Well, hell. Things were just getting better and better.

Harlan ripped the memory stick from the computer without shutting anything down. He forced himself to slowly take off his denim shirt and hang it over the chair, indicating to anyone watching that he planned to come back.

"What are you going to do?"

Harlan didn't answer at first. He stood and pulled the copies from the common printer on his way to the restroom.

"Harlan?"

"Gina, you remember what I said about calling Shaun? Right now I want you to park in front of the coffee shop next door. Back into the space so you can just pull out and drive. Okay? I don't want you to get boxed in by the cops."

"I'll call you in the next five minutes. If I don't call, you leave. You got it? And you call Shaun."

"Harla—"

He hung up and walked into the unisex restroom, shoving the pages he'd copied down the front of his T-shirt. He didn't lock the door.

There was only one toilet and a large shelving unit that occupied the entire back wall. In the far corner Harlan climbed the shelves to get to the ten-foot-high tiled ceiling that extended from the store into the bathroom. He pushed up on a tile and lifted himself into the suspended area.

The space between the roof and the ceiling was about three feet. Metal girders ran parallel to each other about two feet apart. The tiles hung suspended on wires. There was no place for him to put his weight without crashing through to the floor. He would have to hang like a bat.

He reached up for the girder directly overhead and hung upside down, looping his ankles over the metal beam as he replaced the tile exactly as it had been on the metal tracks. He hoped that would slow the cops down a little. Taking a deep breath, he reached up and hung by his hands to crawl hand over hand, monkey-bar style.

He had to go slowly to avoid bumping the wires suspended from each ceiling tile. Insulation, blown in years ago, now flaked off and stuck to his hands and ankles. He was only about fifteen feet from the wall of the coffee shop next door, but his palms were burning by the time he reached it thanks to the fiberglass shards in the insulation.

A thin wall of gympsum board separated him from the next business space. He had no idea whether there was a suspended ceiling in the coffee shop. But there was a steel beam running alongside the wall, so he was able to stop hanging upside down.

He balanced on the lower beam, crouching down in the small space to avoid hitting his head. He fished out his phone and dialed Gina.

She answered on the first ring.

"Are you in front of the coffee shop?" he asked.

"Yes. Where are you?"

"I'm *in* the coffee shop."

"But I'm directly in front of it. I don't see you."

"I'll be right there. Get ready to drive."

He half crawled, half duckwalked to the back of the building on the steel beam, hanging on to the top of the half wall of gypsum board. His hands and ankles started to ooze droplets of blood.

He didn't think about the pain. Instead, he concentrated on reaching the end of the beam. He hoped to hell the back room was a restroom or storeroom.

He counted to five, waiting for the next whir of the coffee grinder to put his feet through the gypsum board. When the machine started, he drew his knees up and pushed out. There was a loud crash as a jagged circle of gypsum board hit a toilet lid.

For once today, something was going right. The coffee shop didn't have suspended ceilings. He'd punched through two layers of drywall separated by several inches of nothing and ended up in another bathroom. He was also grateful the bathroom wasn't in use, particularly as it appeared to be a ladies' room.

His feet dangled in midair. Gypsum plaster dust drifted down like a fine misting of rain as he quickly kicked out more of the drywall so he could fit though the hole. In one motion he moved through the opening and landed beside the toilet, twisting his knee as he hit the marble floor.

Pain radiated up his thigh. But he was in one piece, and no one came crashing through the door. He swept away the worst of the drywall from his clothes and locked the ladies' bathroom door on his way out to Gina and Adam.

"You okay?" she asked. "You're limping."

He nodded, slamming the door and gritting his teeth against the pain in his knee. "Go."

She pulled out of the parking space. "What was on the flash drive?"

"Everything Kate said. From what I saw, Sarah's study proves it all."

"I see." She took a deep breath and put on a brave smile. "All right, then, where's my mocha latte?"

He gave her that *GQ*-cover grin. "Sorry, babe, in all the rush, I forgot. Catch you later?"

She nodded and turned the car toward the airport. "I'm counting on it."

Saturday night

"THEY WHAT?"

"The FBI got a hit on a credit card at a Kinko's for Gina Rodgers. Police got there within ten minutes and surrounded the building. When they went in, the person using the card was gone." The man shuffled nervously back and forth, but the senator was too rattled to enjoy his usual game of making people uneasy. This was not how he'd envisioned things going at all.

"They have security video of a man in a baseball cap using the card at one of the computer stations. When they dusted for prints, they got a hit on Harlan Jeffries from his military file."

"How did he get away?"

"Apparently he crawled through the suspended ceiling into the coffee shop next door."

"Does anyone have a clue where they are now?"

"No, sir," mumbled the aide.

"Then get the hell out of my office!" bellowed the senator.

Jordan Bell leaned back in his seat and took a deep breath. This was not the way things had been planned.

It could not start to fall apart, not now. Too much was at stake. Too much had been carefully put in place.

An incoming call on his private line interrupted his spiraling thoughts.

"Jordan, it's me."

He recognized the voice instantly. "Harlan, where are you? What's going on?"

"I think you might be the one to tell me that. People are trying to either arrest us or set us up for murder. Do you know anything about this?"

"No," Jordan answered without hesitation, but something about his voice must have given him away.

"I don't believe you."

"Where are you? Come in so I can help you."

"Exactly how would you be doing that? I've got to admit you make me nervous right now, Jordan. I get the distinct impression I'm being set up."

"I swear that's not true. Let me help you."

Harlan laughed, but it was a sound completely devoid of humor. "I don't think so."

"Let me see you. I need to speak with you in person."

"I don't trust you right now, J.B."

"I swear. On Jimmy's life, I swear."

There was a long silence. Jordan thought he'd dropped the call. Finally Harlan spoke again. "Okay, we can arrange a meeting."

"When?"

"Soon. I'll be in touch."

"Where are you?"

Dead air was his only reply.

Jordan hung up, poured a glass of scotch and stared at the ceiling. Could it still come together?

Harlan must still have the information he needed. There was no other place it could be. He settled back in his chair to wait.

The next twenty-four hours would make the difference.

Chapter Fourteen

What a difference twenty-four hours could make. Lights whipped by on either side, and Gina felt the pressure forcing her back into the plush leather seat as the plane's wheels left the ground. The angle of the incline was sharp. For a few moments she felt weightless. The tension eased from her body as the pilot leveled out the altimeter.

She had no idea where they were going in D.C. And right now, she didn't care.

Harlan had said, "Shaun's house. We'll be safe for now."

She hadn't asked for more details.

After Harlan's narrow escape from Kinko's, they'd driven to the airport to meet his friend. Gina wasn't sure what kind of plane she'd been expecting but certainly not a corporate Learjet, complete with a stateroom and lounge area. Before leaving Dallas, she'd sat in the bar area and called 9-1-1 from her cell phone to report Tammy's murder anonymously.

Afterward she'd poured herself a large shot of Patron tequila from the bottle under the counter. For the first time in three days she wasn't actively running for her life, and everything she'd lost began to sink in.

Thankfully, Adam had been perfectly happy to curl up in a large leather seat in front of a DVD player. He'd fallen asleep before takeoff with Martin curled up beside him. Gina was free to settle into her own cushy chair and sleep if she wanted. She tried closing her eyes, the droning of the plane's engines the perfect white noise, but found she couldn't unwind.

Harlan was up front in the cockpit with Shaun. "Catching up," he'd said.

Shaun Logan was from Ireland, or so Gina assumed from his lilting accent. He didn't volunteer any information about himself other than his name, although he was friendly enough. He'd told her the flight would take around two and a half to three hours.

Gina tried several positions in her seat before finally giving up and walking to the lounge area again. Harlan was there packing ice in a plastic sack.

"My knee," he explained.

"Come stretch out and put it up," she said. "Don't sit all cramped in the cockpit. That's nuts."

He smiled like a little boy. "That's what Shaun told me, too."

He followed her to the seating area, and she got some pillows to prop up his knee on the glass coffee table.

"Does it hurt?"

He looked at her and dropped the mask for a moment. "Like hell."

"Do you have anything you can take?"

He shook his head.

"What about Shaun and his floating palace?"

He laughed. "This is amazing, isn't it?"

She nodded, looking around at the etched-glass lamps and purple walls.

"Some rock star leases it."

"Really?"

"You thought Shaun owned it?"

"Well, yeah."

"No, he just flies 'em. I think he might have borrowed this one without exactly signing it out."

Three days ago that statement would have had her in a panic. Tonight she only raised an eyebrow.

"Will he get in trouble? Will *we* get into trouble?"

"Compared with the trouble we're already in?" He shook his head. "No, this is pretty minor. He pretty much sits around waiting for these folks to decide if they want to fly somewhere. So the worst that could happen is he may have to manufacture engine trouble if they ask for the plane tonight."

She tried to smile with a nonchalance she wasn't feeling. "Oh, well, if that's all, I won't worry about him." She sank into the recliner beside him.

"Please don't. Shaun is perfectly capable of taking care of himself, believe me."

"That's good. I used to be. Before all this."

"Independence was your middle name, huh?"

"Not always. Not when I was young. It came…later."

She kneaded the pillow as she talked and checked to make sure Adam was still sleeping before going on. Again Harlan listened without any prompting, and that made her want to talk.

"I always wanted to be independent. To take care of me. That's why Sarah and I lost touch after my stepdad died. He'd left everything to Sarah and Adam. She felt horribly guilty about that. I couldn't make her understand that it didn't bother me."

She cleared her throat and rearranged her legs in the seat. "I mean, I wanted to do it on my own. And she needed the money for Adam. But she wanted to share. It's how she thought things should have been all along. We fought about the cabin specifically. That's why we hadn't talked in so long."

She stopped, felt the burning behind her eyes and willed it away. "That seems so silly now. I should've—"

"Stop." He put his hand to her lips. The warmth surprised her. "Don't do that to yourself. The worst words in the English language are *I should have* and *if only*. I'm not saying don't have regrets. Everyone does." He glanced away before looking back at her. "But don't beat yourself up about them."

He smiled sadly and stood to walk away. But she reached for his hand to stop him.

"Wait. Don't leave. I want—" She stopped.

Could she live with no regrets, starting now? This seemed like a heck of time to start. "Sit with me for a while."

He stared at her, his expression unreadable as the smile disappeared, then returned. "What do you want, Gina? Tell me."

"I want to feel safe. I want—" She took a deep breath, could feel her face flushing, but spoke clearly, "You."

"You sure? 'Cause I'm not safe."

She nodded and stared back, willing herself not to look away even as he slid back into the seat beside her and leaned in, touching his lips to hers. Initially his touch was soft, just the barest brush of a kiss.

When she opened her mouth to kiss him back, he pulled her to his chest, inhaling her. She could smell the dust from his trip across the ceiling of the copy store and something deeper as he ran his hands down her back. She felt his heart rate increase and moved to gain better access to his mouth.

An insistent buzzing started in her ears, and before she knew what was happening, he was pulling away, reaching around her, shaking his head. The phone on the table behind her was ringing. She could feel another deep blush starting at the roots of her hair and making its way down her face and neck as he leaned back to talk.

What in the world had she been thinking?

"Yeah." His face was unreadable as he listened to whatever it was the caller was saying.

"Okay, be right there." He hung up the phone and turned back to her. "Shaun needs help. Gotta go." He stood and started to walk away, then stopped for a moment, leaning down to get the bag of ice he'd dropped. "I'm sorry."

For what? Kissing me or stopping?

It was awkward, sitting there looking up at him like that. Gina shrugged. *I kiss hot guys in private airplanes every day.* They both knew that wasn't true.

"No problem," she mumbled.

He nodded and walked away.

Liar. She'd just added one more huge problem on top of all the disasters in this chaos that was her new life—Harlan Jeffries.

ADAM WOKE UP grumpy when the wheels hit the runway. Gina understood how he felt. But Martin licking his face cheered Adam a lot more than it would have cheered her.

At the private airstrip Shaun gave them the keys to a huge blue Hummer. "That's quite a car," said Gina.

Shaun shrugged. "You'll be safe at the house." He carried Adam on his shoulders to the vehicle and gently placed him in the backseat. Harlan's swollen knee was evident even through his jeans now. He was limping despite his protests and the ice pack they'd refilled.

"I don't know how I can ever thank you enough," Gina said.

"There's no need to be thanking me," Shaun returned. "I owe Harlan a debt that can never be repaid."

Shaun took her hand, and for a second or two Gina thought he was going to bow over it. Then he dropped her hand, and the moment was gone. Nodding to Harlan, he left without another word.

Harlan wouldn't tell her any more about who Shaun was or what he did, just that they'd known each other in Iraq and that they indeed "owed each other." Gina quit asking questions after that. She didn't want to know any more tonight, especially when she saw Shaun's house.

She could tell it was beautiful by the light of the full moon. Set back a few yards from the road on a deep wooded lot, Shaun's home was in Tysons Corner, an upscale D.C. suburban neighborhood. The house was a two-story with soaring antebellum columns fronted by a circular drive, lined with stately oak trees. Garbage cans stood like sentinels at the curb.

They walked inside to a showplace, outfitted with antiques and completely updated. Harlan turned on the lights as Adam and Martin galloped through the house together.

It was after eleven. Gina was wiped out and wished her nephew was. But Adam's nap had thrown off his sleep schedule.

"Want Maddie," he demanded.

Gina groaned softly. No way Shaun had *Madagascar* in his DVD collection.

Harlan stepped up to the plate. "Hey, buddy, let's get a bath first. Then we'll find something fun on Shaun's big-screen TV."

"Maddie?"

"I don't know about that, but we'll find something interesting. I promise. Meanwhile, I bet your aunt Gina will fix you something fantastic to eat while you get cleaned up."

He looked to Gina with a hopeful expression and gestured toward the back of the house. "Kitchen's that way. Do you mind figuring out food?"

She shook her head. "No problem. But you're taking a chance. You don't even know if I can cook."

She didn't give him a chance to reply but smiled over her shoulder and headed in the direction he'd pointed.

Actually she was quite grateful to let Harlan deal with Adam and see what she could do about the promised food. She loved to cook. And it had been entertaining to see that slightly panicked look on Harlan's face.

Aunt Gina. This was the first time anyone had called her that besides Sarah. She swallowed hard against threatening tears and wandered toward the kitchen.

Two hours later, Adam was asleep and Gina soaked in a whirlpool tub. Jets whirred softly as she felt the tension ease from her body. There was a television in the bathroom.

Incredible. Was this really Shaun's house or another one of his client loans? She decided she didn't care.

Feeling decadent and mindless, she aimlessly channel surfed using the waterproof remote. Citrus candles scented the air as she sank deeper into frothy bubbles, enjoying a re-airing of her favorite late-night talk show. She glanced at the clock—1:45 a.m.

No wonder everything felt off balance, as if she was playing catch up. She was.

At the same time she realized she was trusting Harlan to keep them safe. For now, that was all that mattered. It surprised her how fast she'd gotten to this point. A week ago it would have frightened her. She didn't trust easily, and to be trusting him when it seemed he had so many secrets... Well, that was scary. But a lot had changed in the past week, and her priorities had rearranged themselves accordingly.

She glanced at the pile of pages on the stool beside the tub. Even with Sarah's study, she had no idea what was going on. Harlan had given her the copies from the flash drive, but she didn't understand most of what she read until the final paragraph.

Ethyl mercury (also known as thimerosal) injected into the developing brain causes severe damage.

That was pretty damn clear, even for someone science challenged like herself. Was this the reason Sarah, Sullivan, Kate and Tammy had died?

She glanced at the pages again and decided it might be worth another read. She took a deep breath and dried her hands on the fluffy towel, even as she wished she'd never heard of thimerosal or ethyl mercury. One more time, and maybe she'd understand what it all meant.

A half hour later she leaned her head back against the rim of the tub, her mind awash with everything she'd just tried to absorb.

Although it was a fairly technical paper, she'd figured out a couple of things. For one, Sarah was pretty darn smart. And two, mercury in vaccines was a really stupid idea. No wonder her sister had been so anxious to get the information to the proper authorities. It seemed pretty important. But had it been worth her life? Gina didn't think so. She'd never think so.

She stood and grabbed a towel, desperately wishing she could forget about everything for a while.

HARLAN SAT ON THE cushioned outdoor sofa icing his knee. He figured he'd done some sort of damage when he jumped out of the ceiling. Hell, he was only thirty-four years old. He'd jumped out of airplanes and been fine. But flattened by jumping eight feet? It was embarrassingly appropriate for the way the day had gone.

He looked at the three pills cradled in his palm. He'd scoured the medicine cabinets in every bathroom of the house and come up with a roll of antacids, a box of sleeping pills, three aspirin and a bottle of Vicodin. The prescription painkiller was out of the question. He couldn't afford to be that incapacitated, no matter how badly his knee hurt.

So even though he knew it would be like spitting in the ocean, he washed down the three aspirin with beer and hoped for the best.

Adam was asleep with Martin stationed at the foot of his bed. Harlan didn't want to know if the dog wasn't fully house-broken. The boy was so attached to the animal right now, there was no question of separating them. Apparently the feeling was mutual.

He leaned back in his seat and lit the Cuban he'd found in his quest for pain medication. Shaun had said to make himself at home, and he had. If he couldn't drink heavily or take the pain meds he'd found, at least he was going to smoke. Anything to get his mind off how much his knee hurt. He'd send his friend a whole new box of cigars when this was over.

He had to tell Gina what was going on. If she didn't hear the truth from him, she'd be furious. It wasn't that Harlan had lied to her, but he hadn't told her the whole story. Initially, it hadn't seemed important and there hadn't been time. But now Sarah was dead, and full disclosure was crucial.

But how could he tell her he had been "assigned" to Sarah. Gina's first question would be "why?" And that was the sticky part.

He was staring at the stars when he heard the glass slider open. Gina stood in the doorway, moonlight illuminating her face. She was wearing a robe she must have found in one of the closets upstairs.

Again he wondered what this might be like if they were here

under different circumstances. Not running for their lives. Not grieving for her sister, her friend. He shook off the improbable direction his thoughts were headed.

Her right eye was a brilliant shade of purple and yellow since her fall in the diner on Wednesday. Her hair was wet, curling around her shoulders, and she was holding the papers he'd printed from the memory stick. Her other hand held the curtains back. He hadn't given her Sarah's letter to Adam. He didn't think she was ready for that yet.

"How's the knee?"

He shrugged and took a sip of the beer. "You want one of these?" he asked, indicating the bottle. "There's white wine in the refrigerator, too." He pointed to a small deck fridge by the barbecue grill. He didn't need her next to him looking like that.

"No, thanks. Is there water?" She headed toward the outdoor kitchenette area.

He watched as she bent over to pick out a plastic bottle. The satin material stretched taut across her butt as she leaned in and he continued to stare, barely tearing his eyes away in time when she turned to sit beside him.

That was not what he'd planned when he'd sent her to the fridge. He'd hoped she'd sit across from him. And he hadn't meant to ogle her, but the woman had a world-class ass. He'd noticed that a couple days ago. He would have had to be dead not to have noticed. As he wrestled with his conscience, he wondered what she was wearing under the robe.

She continued to talk, completely unaware that his thoughts had skittered off into the deep end of the gutter. "One sip of anything alcoholic, and I'll be out like a light." She leaned her head back against the sofa cushion, turning her head to look at him. "I didn't know you smoked."

"Only under special circumstances."

"You mean when you're stressed?"

"Or completely hammered."

She coughed a laugh as she choked on the water. "Right. Me, too."

She looked at him, really looked at him, and something deep inside clicked. Being with her was doing something to him that had nothing to do with sex, but he couldn't figure out what it was.

"Care to guess which case this is?"

She shook her head. "I'll let my imagination do the work. You got another one of those?" She pointed to the cigar.

He didn't know what to say. He was still lost in her last comment.

"You should see your face." She grinned. "I'm joking. I tried one once. Made me sick as a dog, but I do like the way they smell." She held up the papers. "I've been reading this again. I still don't understand the meat of it, but the conclusion's pretty clear."

"You think it would have worked for the Daubert hearing Kate told us about?" He moved in the chair, struggling to keep up with the change of subject and his raging libido. The bag of ice slipped off his knee, falling to the deck with a distinct thud.

"I'm no lawyer, but yeah, I do." She bent to get the bag with one hand before he did and put it back on his leg.

"So what do you want to do with this?" he asked. Her hand on his skin was distracting him.

"I want to get it to Senator Jordan Bell, like Sarah asked me to. But I'm not sure how we're going to do that with everything in the news." She rearranged the ice in the bag until it made a small hollow for his knee.

Here was the place he could tell her. He could say, "Trust me, it's not going to be a problem."

Instead it was, "We'll figure out something. We're going to be okay."

Her hand was still on the bag of ice, and she stopped to look at him with a baffled expression. "You really believe that, don't you?"

He nodded. "Yes, I do."

"Why? How?"

"Because we're going to make it okay."

"God, I've got to love an optimist." She stopped, and he watched as the flush swept up her face. "I didn't mean that the way it sounded."

It was his turn to grin.

She tried changing the subject. "Is Adam asleep?"

He nodded. "Out like a light. Martin may not be much of a watchdog, but he is a sleeping machine."

"Yeah, he seems to work like a sleeping pill. Speaking of which, did you find anything to take for your knee in Shaun's medicine cabinets?"

The ice bag was in her hand again. The ends of her wet hair brushed his thigh as she leaned over his knee and looked at the swelling. The upside to injuring himself was that she was now completely comfortable with touching him.

"Just some aspirin." He spoke around the lump in his throat. "There's some Vicodin upstairs, but it knocks me on my butt. I'll make do with the other."

"You sure?"

"Yeah, I'll be fine."

"I'm starting to notice a pattern here. Is this denial?"

"No, it's the power of positive thinking."

She laughed, a low sexy sound that did something to him, pulling him in and heightening every sense. "Ah, zen optimism. Yeah, that's me." She rolled her eyes, completely unaware of the effect she was having on him.

He didn't say anything. He couldn't, for fear he'd give away what she'd just done. So he looked at her.

"What?" Her eyebrows drew together, and she smiled at him, the laughter still glowing in her eyes. But when she saw his face, she sobered. Her hand was still on his knee, but it fell away as she met his gaze.

"It's good to hear you laugh."

He reached for her hand and pulled it between his palms.

She took a deep breath. "Sitting here with you seems so surreal. A week ago—"

"Both our worlds were totally different." Six days ago he'd wanted her gone. Now the thought of her leaving made him uncomfortable, unsettled. He had to do something to keep her with him..Once he told her the truth, she would leave.

"Harlan, I know this is probably not a—"

"What?" He stared, knowing it would fluster her. But he didn't care. He wanted her the way she'd been on the plane.

He wanted…her. The knowledge had something releasing in his chest that he'd been holding on to since he woke up in a field hospital in Iraq. He pushed away the memory as he brushed the back of his fingers across her cheek.

"—a good time for—" She shook her head.

"For what?" he whispered, leaning toward her.

She didn't back away. Instead she leaned into him. "This." She touched her lips to his, and what started out as a gentle kiss, soon became a take-no-prisoners kind of kiss.

He slid his hands into her damp hair, and she tilted her head to get a better angle on his lips. He inhaled and caught the fresh scent of her shampoo. Her skin was warm, and he'd been cold for so long. Too long.

He had her in his arms and across his lap with his hands inside her robe before they both looked at each other and realized they were still outside on a deck where any neighbor could glance out a window and see them. Of course, the neighbor would have to be looking into their side yard at 2:00 a.m.

He didn't think about what he was asking. What he was changing. "Race you to my room?" He kissed her neck and helped pull the sides of her robe back together.

"What do I get if I beat you there?"

Her eyes were dancing as he left the belt untied.

"I think I might need a head start."

She grinned. "I think you've already got one."

"Well, I am working with an injury."

She looked down at the evidence that he most certainly was not. "Could've fooled me." She mocked a frown and lightly ran her palm from his knee up beyond his thigh.

He exhaled through clenched teeth when her hand reached its destination.

"So you still didn't tell me.... What do I get if I beat you there?" Her breath tickled his ear.

And now they were talking about something completely different.

"You won't." His hand slid back inside her robe, and he decided the neighbors would have to be awake and really looking to be scandalized at two in the morning. She gasped as he brushed his fingertips down the side of her breast. "But I'm sure we can work something out," he said.

"Oh, I'm sure we can. But what if I decide I can't wait to get upstairs?"

He raised an eyebrow and watched as she slipped the robe from her shoulders. She took his breath away. So beautiful, bathed in the moonlight. Her eyes, the lushness of her body. Gina wasn't fashion model thin. She had curves and a figure that he wanted to sink into, and for more than just one night.

The thought startled him, and he didn't say anything for a moment.

Neither of them was looking for a lifetime. He knew he wasn't equipped to provide that, as much as he might wish differently. But would she be here like this, even for tonight, if she knew everything?

She stared at him through the semidarkness and again something shifted, changed.

He'd never know. He smiled and cleared his throat as he reached for her. "Then I guess we'll have to improvise." Wrapping his arms around her waist, he pulled her to him. "But don't worry, I think fast on my feet."

Her soft laughter washed over him, washing away the reservations he had about the rightness of what was about to happen. It was so damn good to finally hear her laugh.

"I've no doubt you'll come up with something," she murmured.

He banished any thoughts of remorse as he leaned in to kiss his way down her neck. "Just you watch," he said.

"As long as you don't make me wait."

Chapter Fifteen

Sunday morning

Gina lay in bed listening to the shower. She didn't want to open her eyes yet. She knew it was early. Probably close to seven.

What she really wanted was to roll over and go back to sleep, particularly since she hadn't slept much last night. She smiled to herself. That hadn't exactly been a hardship.

Wow was all she could think.

Her mind was still too fuzzy to come up with any other word. It had been a long time for her. Two years in fact.

Wow. Her body was still zinging.

Clay had never had much of a wow factor. This was pretty, well…wow.

She'd be more coherent after she had coffee. She gave in and opened her eyes, blinking against the light streaming in through the windows of the bedroom. Her robe was at the foot of the bed, where she'd left it last night after the race upstairs.

She wasn't sure who'd gotten to the room first. Didn't matter. They'd both won.

A morning news show was on television, muted. She would have ignored it, but a familiar logo and tagline filled the screen. She scrambled for the remote on the bedside table.

A Cure for All the Scourges of Tomorrow was emblazoned in tall blue letters across the screen.

That was the tagline she'd proposed for PharmaVax's new ad campaign exactly one week ago. How had it gotten out there so fast? Pulling the sheet around her, she punched up the volume.

"PharmaVax was given a huge shot in the arm last night when Senate bill 1237 was introduced to Congress by Senator Jordan Bell of Mississippi, head of the Congressional Vaccine Safety Committee. Despite strong opposition from Senator Sandra Hall of Texas, the proposed legislation will grant the company blanket immunity from liability for the production of its new Indonesian flu vaccine."

The cameras switched to footage of the senator being interviewed as he left some kind of formal dinner. His black tie and tails were quite debonair in the camera's glow. Gina didn't think she'd ever seen him live on camera before. She'd simply heard his name in the news.

His voice held the slow, honeyed tones of the Deep South. "We feel it is incumbent upon us to ensure that companies like Pharma-Vax are protected from frivolous lawsuits that would keep them from pursuing the medicines and vaccines that our society needs— particularly the vaccine for H3N6, otherwise known as the Indonesian flu. PharmaVax is very close to a viable vaccine for this disease that could produce a worldwide pandemic. By granting the company this liability waiver, PharmaVax can go forward with their research in a more timely fashion and provide the protection that we as a nation and ultimately the world needs."

Gina felt the remote tumble from her fingers. Jordan Bell was behind the vaccine liability waiver? If that were the case, he wouldn't want anything to do with Sarah's study.

She stood and pulled the top sheet from the mattress with a snap. She had to talk to Harlan. They had to change plans. Jordan Bell was the last person they should be giving Sarah's study to.

She marched into the bathroom before she thought it through. She didn't stop to think that she might be infringing on Harlan's privacy.

He was still in the shower. Steam billowed at the ceiling. He was humming to himself. She saw him through the glass door, but he couldn't hear her over the running water.

"Harlan!"

"What?" He stuck his head out of the enclosure. Shampoo was plastered around his ears. He looked like a little boy until he turned those potent gray eyes on her. He went from being a cute boy to a hot guy, and despite the mess they were in, her heart did a little flip as she looked at him.

"There's something I've got to talk to you about."

"Yeah?"

"There was something on the news." Standing in her sheet, she was suddenly shy and felt silly for having barged into his shower. This could wait three minutes for him to get the soap out of his eyes. "I'm sorry. I can wait for you out here."

He had a puzzled expression. "You sure?"

"Yeah." She nodded and scurried out of the bathroom before the blush worked its way up her cheeks. She wasn't sure why, but she was embarrassed. She reached for her robe at the end of the bed.

The newscaster had moved on to another story about a charity function at Lincoln Center in New York City. The camera panned a ballroom scene with tuxedo-clad men and designer-gowned women.

"Last night the talk of the town was Francesca Ria, a soprano from Italy who really knows how to hit the high notes." Gina reached out to flip off the television as she belted her robe. Her hand froze as she looked at the well-dressed attendees. Something about the scene bothered her, something at the edge of her memory, but she couldn't place it.

Harlan's cell phone jangled on the bedside table. Pachelbel's Canon in D Major. Gina loved that piece. Sarah had it played at her wedding. Seemed odd to hear it as a cell phone ring tone, especially Harlan's. He didn't seem the classical music type.

She wasn't sure what made her do it. Maybe it was feeling unsure of herself or because Harlan seemed so mysterious and she was curious. But she picked up the phone to look at the caller ID. And just like that, her world turned upside down.

Jordan Bell was listed as the caller.

Her fingers felt numb. How could he have this number? Why would he be calling Harlan?

She stared blankly at the television. The tuxedo-clad attendees were still on-screen.

A memory clicked. A picture on Harlan's mantel. A familiar face in a wedding photo.

God, that had been Jordan Bell. *Harlan knew Jordan Bell.*

She let the newfound knowledge sink in. Did that mean Harlan worked for Jordan Bell?

The phone continued ringing. The shower stopped. He would be able to hear the ring tone now.

She punched the End button and put the phone back on the bedside table as the door to the bathroom opened. Her stomach churned. Harlan came in with a towel wrapped around his waist and another slung around his neck.

"Sorry, I couldn't hear you earlier." His smile seemed sincere as he crossed the room and pulled her into his arms. "Good morning."

His chest was warm and still damp from the shower. He was about to kiss her when he saw her face. "What is it?"

She had no idea how to fake this. God, it was happening too fast. Her mouth was dry as dust. She couldn't even swallow.

"I…I needed to tell you about something that I saw on the new—"

A yap and a thud from across the hall interrupted her. Adam shouted, "No, doggie! No!"

She tried not to heave an audible sigh of relief.

"Martin," Harlan muttered under his breath. "Hang on, I'll be right back."

He dropped the towel without any self-consciousness and pulled on his jeans and T-shirt on his way out the door. Gina stood there for about twenty seconds after the door closed, her mind racing.

Harlan worked for Jordan Bell. That explained so much.

How could she have been such an idiot? *Gina the Screwup strikes again.* Lord, this was about as royally screwed up as it got.

So what was he doing here with her besides the obvious? God, she'd slept with him. How could she have been so stupid?

That thought alone drove her to action. She didn't allow herself the luxury of tears. Not now. Later she'd have a terrific screaming fit. She'd have time to throw up, too. Right now she had to hurry.

Two minutes later she was in her own room, pulling on her clothes and formulating a plan.

HARLAN ZIPPED HIS BAG and checked his phone. Jordan had called again. He had to call him back.

He didn't want to. He didn't want to hear his mentor's reasons for selling out. Didn't want to tell him where he was or deal with the mess that he'd just made of the situation with Gina. He'd certainly complicated matters last night. Before, he'd just thought Gina would be mad. Now she was going to be livid when she found out the truth.

He could smell the scent of bacon and eggs wafting up the staircase. He might as well start explaining. This was going to take a while.

She was pouring coffee when he hobbled into the kitchen. Adam had parked himself in front of the living-room television with Martin.

"Something smells great," he said, attempting to break the ice.

He sat at the table and propped up his knee. The situation felt awkward. Something had happened when he'd walked into the bedroom after his shower. They weren't comfortable together anymore. He was about to tank that comfort level anyway, but he found himself missing it already.

Gina turned around. "I have lattes, sort of." She grinned and pressed one of the mugs into his hand, dropping a kiss on his temple as she made her way to the stove. He frowned at her back, wondering if he'd completely misread the situation earlier upstairs.

"Great." He took a big sip and hid a grimace. She'd added lots of sugar, but that didn't hide the bitter flavor of the coffee.

"How does it taste?"

He nodded. "It's good."

She wrinkled her nose. "You're not a very good liar. It's too bitter. I don't know what kind of coffee Shaun buys, but it's some kind of strong." She took a small sip from her own mug. "You want more sugar?"

He shook his head. "No, this is fine." He took another deep swallow, draining half the mug. "It's okay. Really. I'll take caffeine any way I can get it."

She watched him as he drank, an inscrutable expression on her face.

"You want toast with your eggs?"

"Only if you've got it already made."

"No problem." She put a plate in front of him filled with food and walked a tray into the other room, calling over her shoulder. "I thought Adam would enjoy getting to eat in front of the television." She returned and sat across from him with only a coffee mug.

"You're not eating?" He sipped more coffee.

"Not hungry, but you go ahead. I thought we'd chat."

He stopped with the fork halfway to his mouth. That didn't sound good. He took another shot of coffee and drained the mug.

She smiled, but this time the expression was cold and didn't reach her eyes. "I'll get you a refill." She was at the counter getting the stainless steel coffee pot and asked, "When were you going to tell me?"

"Tell you what?"

She turned to glare at him. "That you worked for Jordan Bell."

Chapter Sixteen

Harlan pressed his lips together and nodded as his heart rate kicked up a notch. "When did you figure that out?"

"This morning. There was a news story, and then he called you on your cell phone."

Harlan concentrated on keeping his face blank as he set the fork on the side of his plate. The motion sent his napkin cascading to the floor, and he bent to pick it up. He was stalling, thinking this had to be the worst possible way for the situation to be unfolding.

When he straightened, he realized the situation *had* gotten worse. Gina wasn't holding the coffee pot any longer but a gun that was pointed at him. His own gun.

"Where did you get that?" he asked, even though he knew exactly where she had found it. Under the mattress in their, rather, his bedroom.

"Did you kill Sarah?" she asked. Her voice wasn't steady, but her hands were.

"Gina, calm down."

"I am calm, but don't treat me like a fool, Harlan. You know where I got this gun. There were only a couple of places you could hide it that would be childproof and where you could reach it in a hurry. I watched you do it in the hotel, remember?"

He shook his head. "You surprise me."

"You're not the only one with secrets. I surprise a lot of people." She squared her shoulders. "Did you kill Sarah?"

"No. Did you really think that?" No wonder she was pointing the Glock at him.

"I never went into your garage in Starkville. I didn't think you could have done it, but I'm not sure anymore. You could have gone back in the afternoon, after Kate and the diner."

"You don't believe that." He was surprised, but knew he shouldn't have been. By his not telling her the whole truth, he'd thrown everything he'd done since she'd known him under a cloud of suspicion.

She threw an arm out in exasperation, and her dark curls danced against the white T-shirt she wore. "I don't know what to believe. You've lied to me several times now."

"I swear to you, I never harmed Sarah. I was there to keep her safe." As soon as the words left his mouth, he knew he'd said the wrong thing.

Her eyes filled. "Well, you did a crappy job, Harlan, let me tell you."

He felt the accusation like a body blow. He deserved her scorn and so much more. "I know that."

She looked toward the den, where Adam was watching television, and motioned with the gun. "Get up. We're going upstairs."

"What?"

"We're not talking down here. I don't want him to overhear this. See, I've learned lots of things from you." Her tone dripped with sarcasm. She was referring to that first night when he wouldn't let the Starkville police talk to them in front of Adam.

"We're going upstairs." Her hands were shaking now, but the gun was big enough that her aim wouldn't have to be that great to blow a good size hole in him.

He stood and walked slowly across the kitchen. She didn't speak to him until they were in one of the guest rooms upstairs. Thankfully it wasn't the one in which they'd spent the night together. He didn't think either of them could handle that.

She had a death grip on the Glock, but he could have told her not to worry. He wasn't going to wrestle her to the ground for it, not with Adam in the house. He wouldn't take the chance. There were hollow points alternating with full-metal jackets in the clip. Those would go through a wall like a hot knife through butter. He'd do whatever she said. He didn't want any of them hurt.

She motioned for him to sit on the bed, so he propped his knee up and leaned against the headboard. She stood several feet away in the doorway, waiting until he was situated to ask her next question.

"Why didn't you tell me that you worked for Jordan Bell? All this time I've been worried about how we'd get the information to him and how I'd talk with him. You never said anything about knowing him."

He didn't answer. She was on a roll and obviously didn't expect him to say anything.

"Do you know what he did last night? It was on the news. Jordan Bell just presented a bill to the Congress offering vaccine liability protection to PharmaVax for the manufacture of their new Indonesian flu vaccine."

Harlan sat up straight as the shock coursed through him. "What? No. That can't be right."

Had Jordan lied about everything, from the very beginning?

"Don't look so surprised. You've been working for him, helping ensure it happened. Making sure Sarah's study never saw the light of day. You must have had a heart attack when I found that memory stick."

"No, Gina, that's not true. I didn't know about any vaccine liability waiver."

"No? Well, let me tell you about it. Senate bill 1237. No liability for any and all damages PharmaVax's new miracle vaccine may cause. God, no wonder y'all were so anxious to get your hands on Sarah's study info. You wanted it buried. I still don't understand how he could do such a thing, but it's obvious Sarah's study could shut down Senator Bell's proposed legislation."

Harlan held up his hands. "Gina, you've got to believe me, that was not what I was sent to do."

"Sent to do?" The fury in her voice became palpable. "Harlan, there is no way in hell I'll believe anything you tell me right now. I don't believe you wanted to hurt her, but after all the lies, I don't trust you."

"What are you going to do?"

"Well, as much as it pains me, you're going to get some relief from your knee problems for a while."

"What?"

She gripped the gun a little tighter and pulled a prescription bottle from her jeans pocket. He recognized the bottle as the one from the medicine cabinet down the hall.

Vicodin. With a sinking feeling he knew what she'd done before she said anything. Now the bittersweet latte made sense.

Hell, he'd drained the damn mug.

"You didn't." He shook his head. Damn pain meds. God, he hated the things. Hated the way they made him feel, made him talk.

"We both know I can't tie you up and keep holding this gun. You'd take it away from me in a heartbeat, so I had to incapacitate you. Honestly, this was the only way I could think of to do it." She pulled a chair from under the vanity across the room and sat down.

"How many?" he asked.

"Four."

"Four? Are you trying to kill me?"

"No, but I can't have you following us either. It won't kill you. At least I don't think so. The bottle says two. It should just make you very sleepy." She shrugged and tried to sound callous. "But if it does do anything worse, it's better than you deserve."

He swallowed, his mouth suddenly dry. He was light-headed as well, but that was too quick for the meds. This was more about dreading what was going to happen when they kicked in.

"We'll just sit here until you're feeling the effects."

He saw her finger tighten on the trigger and looked in her eyes. She was quite serious about this.

"Where's the memory stick?" she asked. "I'd rather not have to go through your pockets after you're asleep."

"Right hip pocket. Can I give it to you?"

She nodded and held the gun with both hands. "Slowly."

He reached into the back pocket of his jeans and pulled out the silver thumb drive, gently laying it on the bed beside him. She raised the gun a bit higher.

He thought about rushing her and took another look at her face. Nothing there but sheer determination. No fear. He remembered her in downtown Dallas with the security guard trying to tow her car right after finding out about Sarah's death. She'd do whatever it took.

"Do you really think this is going to work?" he asked.

"I have no idea. But I can't stay with you. I'm certain that won't work."

"I was going to tell you," he started.

"Yeah, right." She was trying to look bored, but he knew she couldn't help but listen. She had to pay attention until the meds took effect if she was going to keep him from getting that gun from her.

"I was working for Jordan."

She'd obviously come to the same conclusion. She couldn't ignore him. He just wasn't sure how long he would be coherent.

"Well, we've got some time. Go ahead. Why were you working for Jordan?"

He focused on her eyes as he spoke. "He's been family to me for a long time. His son Jimmy and I met in high school. We went to West Point together. Hell, Jordan got me into West Point."

"You never told me you were an officer."

"Yeah, well. I'm not anymore, so it didn't seem very important." *That part of my life is over.* "Jimmy loved being a Marine. And Jordan…Jordan hated that he loved it so much. With his connections, he could have gotten Jimmy stationed someplace safe. But his son wouldn't hear of it.

"We were in Iraq together. Twice. We'd been there twenty-three months total, and we were on our last mission. Hell, we even knew what time our transport flight was taking off stateside."

He felt the first hazy bump from the medicine as it slowly started to kick in. Were the drugs really taking effect that quickly, or was he talking because he finally had an excuse to tell her the truth? Either way he couldn't stop himself from talking.

"We were there to take out a group of al-Qaeda operatives, but a busload of kids got in the way, and Jimmy tried to save them. He didn't make it. He and those kids got blown to hell by several roadside IEDs. I did what I was told, and everybody died. Everybody except the terrorists. They walked away completely unscathed."

He leaned back against the headboard and talked to the ceiling. "I'll never be able to make up for that. So I took my medical discharge and swore I'd never be in that position again." He took a deep breath and looked over at Gina holding the gun. "But damn it, here I am again. Everybody died because I did what I was told to do."

He felt like he was sitting on the shrink's couch back at the military hospital. He shook his head to clear it as best he could and stared at Gina. His vision was starting to blur.

"When I got home, I was pretty messed up. Jordan came to see me. He'd been like a father to me, and we were both grieving. I felt so damn guilty about Jimmy and those kids. J.B. encouraged me to take some classes at State. Use the GI bill. He told me about Sarah needing help with Adam. That's how I ended up meeting your sister."

"You just happened to meet her?"

"Jordan introduced us. I was looking for something to give my life purpose, so I jumped at the opportunity to work with Adam. I never knew about the study or any of Jordan's connections with PharmaVax until the night Sarah disappeared."

"What do you mean?" She was still gripping the gun with both hands.

"After I reported her missing, before you got to Starkville, I called Jordan. I wanted his help with getting the police to take Sarah's disappearance seriously. Remember they were making me wait twenty-four hours before they'd even get involved. Jordan told me that Sarah was working for him, and he was worried something had happened to her. He asked me to watch out for you and Adam. But that's all he would tell me."

"So that's why she told me in her voice mail to take the information to him."

"Yes." He tried to focus on her face, but it was blurring around the edges.

"Why did he think something might have happened to her?"

"Jordan told me people he *owed* were upset by the work Sarah was doing."

"People he owed?" Gina's eyes widened. "Who do you think that is? The people of PharmaVax? My God, that would certainly make sense. He had it wired from the very beginning. Why did he do that?"

Harlan tried shaking his head, but had to grip the side of the bed so he wouldn't fall out of it. His words were beginning to slur. "Don't know. Politics, money, take your pick."

"So, you knew something was going on that first night we met. That someone, probably from the pharmaceutical company, was after us."

"Yes, but I didn't know who." His vision was starting to go. "I'd just talked to him when I found you on the floor at Sarah's. I didn't know what to believe. He'd asked me to stay with Adam until they found Sarah. Then you got there and we found Kate."

He felt his neck wobble back and forth. "I think that's what threw it off track. They never counted on Sullivan. That's what stirred things up so."

"Why did you go along with it after Kate died?"

Even in his drugged haze, he knew that was a good question. Why had he agreed to do the thing he'd sworn he'd never do? Take bad orders, put himself in that kind of position of vulnerability again. Why was he still doing this after so long?

He leaned his head back and didn't answer for a moment. He bit down on the inside of his cheek, hoping the pain would help clear his head. The answer was simple and not so simple. Why had he done this? There had been places along the way he could have stopped but he hadn't.

He swallowed. "To take care of Adam." *And you.*

It was part of what he'd been looking for since he'd gotten home from overseas. This had seemed a way of making up for Jimmy, those kids on the bus. "After Sarah disappeared, I had no idea what would happen to him. Then you arrived and everything fell apart."

But it went deeper than that. He'd been looking for more than that when he'd agreed to stay. He'd wanted his life to mean something.

"What I didn't know about was the vaccine liability waiver Jordan planned. That puts everything in a completely different light. He lied to me too, Gina."

She didn't believe him. He could tell from the sneer on her face. Hell, he wouldn't have believed himself. How had he screwed this up so horribly? All he'd wanted to do was help.

"Yeah, if only I believed you." She stood and seemed to waver in the sunlight streaming in through the wooden blinds. He squeezed his eyes closed. His arms and legs felt like they were floating.

"I don't know how to convince you." *And I sure as hell can't save you.*

Had he said that out loud? He wasn't sure. He opened his eyes again. There were two Ginas standing before him.

"I never wanted you to save me." She drifted toward him, and for a moment he thought he felt her hand on his forearm.

Well, obviously he had said that out loud. He tried to sit up straight, but it was hopeless. There was something he needed to tell her about— What?

Damn, he couldn't remember. Last night? No, it was something else. But it wouldn't stay in his mind long enough for him to form the words.

His tongue was heavy and his speech slurred. "Gina, you and Adam…need…to get out."

"Does Senator Bell know we're here?"

"Don't know." His head lolled back on the headboard as he tried to nod. His body felt weightless, but his heart was heavier than lead. He could smell the floral shampoo she'd used last night. Her head was level with his as she bent to pick up the memory stick from the bed. Her hand brushed his. "Sorry... didn't...tell...sooner."

"Me, too." Her breath was soft on his cheek.

Then his eyes closed, and everything went black.

Chapter Seventeen

Gina watched Harlan's head loll back against the headboard. How had it come to this? She couldn't believe that just hours ago they'd been naked in each other's arms. She dropped the gun on the bed.

Her hands shook as she wiped the back of her knuckles across her eyes. To think for even a moment she'd stood a chance of working something out with him proved her lack of judgment knew no bounds. She stared at him, hoping he'd eventually wake from the Mickey Finn she'd concocted in the kitchen.

She had no idea how long he'd be out. Picking up the gun, she went in search of something to tie his hands and feet. A roll of duct tape from a junk drawer in the kitchen was the only thing she could find.

She checked on Adam again. He was deeply involved in *Sesame Street* and appeared to be happy. She had to make sure he didn't see Harlan like this. The man, snake that he was, mattered to the boy.

That's what was making this so horrible. Harlan was so damn important to Adam. How was she going to deal with that?

She found the end on the duct tape and trussed Harlan up as best she could, mentally scoffing at herself as she eased a pillow under his knee. Why the hell was she bothering to see to his comfort now? With his training she wasn't sure if she was making it ridiculously easy for him to escape. Or perhaps he'd be stuck until someone came to the house?

A chill shimmied down her spine. He had said she needed to get out of here. Could they be on their way even now? She tamped down the fear, unsure of who "they" were. Her hands still trembled but not like they had earlier.

It was almost 8:00 a.m. God, she was past tired. She took one last look at Harlan, sleeping peacefully for the first time since she'd met him—except his feet and hands were bound with silver duct tape.

If only… No, even he'd told her those were words not to be contemplated. She backed away and ran across the hall to pack. She and Adam had to get far away from here. Now.

Twenty minutes later everything was in the car and she'd made her phone calls. She looked at the clock, wondering if she dared take five more minutes. There was one more thing she wanted to know.

She sat in front of Shaun's laptop, trying to figure the odds on whether she still had a backdoor into her account at Dixon Meyers. Given the mass exodus Clay had instigated on Friday afternoon, she figured the chances were pretty good she could still get into the system.

But could the activity be traced? She only had to scoop up Adam and Martin to leave the house. It wouldn't take her long to find what she was looking for, and Harlan's being here shouldn't matter. Within two minutes she was dialed in with full access to the office network.

PharmaVax. She rifled past a couple of PDF files, two annual reports and a Research and Development brochure the marketing folks had e-mailed to her when Dixon Meyers had been developing the ad campaign. The news report had said PharmaVax was developing one vaccine for the Indonesian flu. But something about that niggled at her memory—something from the tour she'd taken of the facility when she'd been in Chicago for one of the advertising meetings at PharmaVax headquarters.

One of the marketing people had taken her into a lab in the R&D portion of the facility. They'd chatted briefly about future products with one of the scientists. Nothing said was confidential. She'd just been getting a feel for the people who worked there as she created a campaign strategy.

But the comments the scientist had made were so interesting that she'd typed up some of the details of their conversation on the plane ride home. She opened the document and felt her eyes widen as she read her own notes from two months before.

A cure for all the scourges of tomorrow. Thirty vaccines are on track to be produced over the next ten years.

She remembered now. Her PharmaVax slogan was born on the flight back to Dallas. She'd used the scientist's own words. But more than that she focused on the number of vaccines. Thirty of them were in PharmaVax's R&D pipeline. Apparently, the vaccine liability waiver Jordan Bell was sponsoring was pretty damn important, not just for the Indonesian flu but for all the scourges of tomorrow.

She printed off her notes and shut down Shaun's computer. Her activity might or might not be traceable. If it was, she intended to be long gone before anyone came looking for her.

TWO HOURS LATER Gina stood in front of a gas station rest room mirror, trying to decide if the haircut she'd just given herself looked okay. It was ragged in places, but the curls leapt around her face and kept the cut from looking too horrible. At least she hoped that was the case.

Adam snuffled occasionally and played with the water faucet in the sink. He was still upset with her. His golden curls lay all around on the floor. She'd given him a combination mullet and buzz cut. While not very attractive, the hairstyle rendered him unrecognizable from the Amber Alert photo on the news.

He'd howled like a banshee, and she'd been grateful for the roadside construction so no one could hear him. Yesterday Harlan had mentioned something about tactile defensiveness. She'd certainly gotten to see that up close and personal.

Martin sniffed about on the floor among all the hair, seemingly baffled at finding Adam's scent there. She didn't even want to think about what else the dog was finding.

She'd forgone makeup to highlight the purples and yellows she was still sporting around her right eye from her fall in the diner. She looked like she'd been in a bar fight. For better or worse, she, too was completely unrecognizable from the woman in the television photos.

"Adam, it's time to go." She gathered up the boy and dog and packed them into Shaun's car.

They met "Sheila" in a McDonald's parking lot a few blocks away. The women's crisis hotline she'd found in the yellow pages at Shaun's had given Gina the woman's number and assured her that Sheila could help them find a safe place to stay. The idea of deceiving women who were running from shattered relationships seemed abhorrent to Gina, but she didn't know where else to turn. A shelter for battered women and children seemed to be one place Harlan and Jordan Bell would not think to look for her and Adam.

Sheila took one look at Gina's face and got right down to business, offering them a place outside of town.

"We usually have two to three women there, but this past week our last two residents moved on to new homes." The older woman smiled. "And much better lives. We keep the refrigerator stocked, and there's a phone, but the number is always blocked on outgoing calls."

Gina was able to stick pretty much to the truth. A man was, in fact, after her and trying to kill her. She just made it sound as if Harlan was the boyfriend who'd given her the black eye. And she'd told Sheila her name was Kara.

She told the truth about Adam. It was too confusing otherwise. Her sister was dead, and she was caring for her autistic nephew. She'd stumbled over that last part badly.

An hour later she was following Sheila through pastureland and dense woods to a comfortable farmhouse nestled in a small forest. An idyllic setting. Gina and Adam were given a large private room right off the kitchen with two twin beds.

Adam was cranky and tired, still in shock. Gina hoped they'd be able to stay in one place for at least twenty-four hours. She had to have time to think, to put together everything she'd learned this morning.

Martin curled up beside Adam on the bedspread. The dog appeared to be worth his weight in gold as he soothed a grumpy Adam, then snuggled in beside the boy and lulled him to sleep. The altercation concerning Dickens was long forgotten; Adam tucked the dinosaur under one arm and the dog under the other.

Gina lay on the other mattress and tried not to think about everything that had just happened. She wasn't able to process it clearly yet. It had all been so fast.

Jordan Bell was trying to push a bill through Congress for a vaccine liability waiver. But why would a U.S. senator go to bed with a pharmaceutical company? It had to be money or politics, just as Harlan had said.

And why had PharmaVax killed Sarah? Because she had a study that could prove very damaging to them both politically and in public opinion. A study proving that thimerosal was very harmful to the developing brain. If that information were released to the public, PharmaVax would not get its vaccine liability waiver and Sullivan's lawsuit would have unleashed a landslide of civil lawsuits against vaccine manufacturers.

Why was PharmaVax after her? Because the company thought she had the study.

Why would they think that? Either because—and she hated to think about this part—Sarah told them before she died, or somehow they got her voice mail. Electronic eavesdropping was a possibility. These were extraordinarily well-funded folks. Or it made more sense that they'd been bugging her or Sullivan's phone.

Now to the hardest part. Why was Harlan working for Jordan? Money? Power? Guilt?

She certainly understood the latter. Jordan was his dead friend's father. It was obvious that Harlan still felt horribly guilty about what had happened in Iraq. Had all his participation really been about trying to assuage the guilt?

None of the traditional answers made sense, unless he'd been telling the truth back there under the influence of those pain pills. If Harlan was working for PharmaVax, he knew that she didn't have the study until they found Dickens's memory stick together. She sat up in the bed.

He couldn't have been working for PharmaVax, or he never would have given her the pages from the copy shop. Had he been telling the truth this morning?

She wasn't sure, but she had zero faith in her judgment right now. It had been so severely lacking up to this point. Sleeping with Harlan had certainly shown her that. She still couldn't believe she'd been such an idiot.

A soft knock on the door interrupted her private pity party. Sheila stood on the threshold with a cup of steaming tea.

"Is there anything you need, Kara?" she asked softly. "I'm about to leave for the afternoon."

Gina came to the doorway. "No, we're fine. Thank you so much." She took the tea. "For everything. I think just knowing we're in a safe place is going to make a big difference for Adam."

"It will—you'll see."

"I don't know. Adam's autism is pretty overwhelming. With all that's happened, he needs some professional help. I'm way out of my league here."

"I understand." Sheila smiled knowingly. "I might be able to help you with that. We've got a child psychologist on staff. I'll see if she could come out and talk with y'all. You're safe now. That's the important thing. One step at a time. This was a big step for you both."

You have no idea.

Chapter Eighteen

Harlan woke to a darkened room and a raging headache that felt like the worst tequila hangover of his life. He could hear his cell phone ringing in his pocket, but he couldn't get to it even if he'd been so inclined.

His feet and hands were trussed like a hog roasting over a fire pit. His knee was swollen to the size of a large grapefruit and hurt like hell. He ignored all that as he shimmied off the bed in search of something, anything, to cut the duct tape.

His hand slid across a small, sharp object in the carpet that stuck in his palm. Hell, it just kept getting better and better. He went down the staircase on his butt like a deranged inchworm and ended up in the kitchen. Bracing himself, he stood by the knife block and raked his hands across a dull eight-inch blade till he hacked through the tape. His hands tingled painfully as the blood began to circulate through his fingers again.

What time was it? The clock read 4:00 p.m.

God, where was she?

He sat back down on the floor and unwrapped his feet, taking precious minutes to let the blood flow back to his toes so he wouldn't fall on his ass when he started moving again. He hurried upstairs, pulling the cell phone from his pocket.

There were half a dozen calls from J.B. That last one had been from him, too. No doubt Jordan was frantic to talk to Harlan.

Of course, Gina and Adam were long gone. Hell. Harlan hadn't expected to find them still here. He'd screwed that up beyond repair by not telling her the truth from the beginning. Or at least not telling her after they'd found out about Sarah.

That seemed to be his forte in relationships, screwing them up beyond repair. He couldn't blame her, but he was scared to death for her. Things were about to go completely berserk, and he wasn't going to be there to keep her and Adam safe. It was his worst nightmare scenario.

He went to Gina's bedroom. A pad of paper was beside the phone with a metro phone book underneath. Car doors slammed outside. He leaned across the bed to peek out the blinds. A dark sedan was parked in the drive, and two hulking men stood beside the hood. This did not look good.

He was out of time. Still he stared at the phone for a moment before picking up the handset and hitting the Redial button. Dates and times were listed next to the numbers that had been called. Two calls had been placed today.

But to whom?

The doorbell rang. Multiple times. After a moment the front door opened. He heard voices in the foyer as he hit Redial on the second number back. The call was picked up on the first ring.

"Fairfax County Women's Crisis Center. May I help you?"

Bingo.

He hung up without saying anything and went to the next number, hitting Redial again.

"You've reached the voice mail for Sheila Levitz. Please leave a message at the tone, and I'll get back to you."

He didn't follow the instructions but hung up when he heard footsteps on the staircase. He scrolled back, scribbling down the two phone numbers he'd dialed. Then he hit Delete on the handset memory and went to the doorway of the bedroom.

He looked around. He had nothing. Gina had taken his gun. The adrenaline kicked in as he took a deep breath.

Showtime.

"Harlan Jeffries? You here?"

There was no place to hide, and with his knee in the shape it was, he couldn't even pretend to fight. He was going to have to tap-dance and probably get the crap beaten out of him, if not worse.

"Yeah, up here." His voice was raspy.

He caught a glimpse of himself in the bureau mirror and grimaced. Hair standing straight up. Bloodshot eyes. Combined with the stubble on his chin and wrinkled clothes, he looked like he'd been out on a bender.

The first man appeared at the top of the stairs, looking as if he'd just stepped out of an Armani trunk show. He wore a deep blue suit with that distinctive bulge under the left shoulder. No amount of tailoring, no matter how fine the suit, could hide some concealed weapons. "Harlan Jeffries?"

"Right. That's me. Who the hell are you?"

"Senator Bell sent us. He's very concerned about you, Ms. Rodgers and the child." He took in Harlan's appearance. "What happened to you?"

"What didn't?" Harlan snarled. "How did you find me?"

"Someone used a computer here to access files at Dixon Meyers Advertising. We traced it. Took us a while, but obviously—" his voice took on a slight sneer "—you needed the rest." Blue Suit pulled a gun from under his jacket and directed Harlan down the stairs. "Let's go, we need to chat."

No way to argue with that. He had no weapon. Nothing but a pounding headache and a trick knee. He hobbled down the stairs to the living room.

Blue Suit didn't waste any time. "Where are Ms. Rodgers and the child?"

Harlan didn't answer and tensed up as thug number two came in from the kitchen, dressed in an identical suit, this one gray, with an identical concealed weapon at the left shoulder. He'd obviously been searching the garage.

"Shaun Logan's been a good friend to you, hasn't he?" said

Blue Suit. "You two served together in Iraq. You've known each other for a while. Loaned you his house. Loaned you his car, too. Right?"

Harlan didn't reply.

"But Ms. Rodgers has it now, doesn't she?"

Harlan shook his head. "I don't know if she still does or not. Gina freaked when she saw Jordan on the news with his liability waiver. She took the boy and left. I don't know where she is."

Blue Suit smiled. "It's all right. We'll find her."

Gray Suit spoke up. "What car does she have?"

Harlan didn't reply.

"Let me save you some time. Is it the blue Hummer or the red Audi?"

"Audi's in the garage," supplied Gray Suit.

Blue smiled again, but the expression didn't reach his eyes. "Fine, so it's the Hummer." He pulled out his cell phone. "Yeah, the car is registered to a Shaun Logan. Blue Hummer. It has OnStar. Someone should be able to hack into the system. If not, contact the company. Tell them his daughter took it for a joyride and he doesn't want the police involved." He hung up and nodded to the man in gray.

The first blow caught Harlan unawares; he'd been focused on that phone call. They were going to find Gina and the car. He wasn't braced for the punch and felt the air whoosh out of his lungs as he doubled over.

"Where's the study, Harlan?" Gray Suit's voice was soft but menacing.

That really hurt. He was down on the rug, close to the window that faced the front of the house. Moving marginally closer to the right, he held on to the sofa arm to stand. He fought for breath and stared at Gray Suit. The man had dead eyes. Harlan had seen eyes like that more times than he cared to remember.

"I have no idea what you're talking about."

"Does Gina have it?" Gray Suit hit him again, three rabbit

punches to his kidney. The pain radiated across his abdomen and up his back. He'd be peeing red for a week.

"Don't know what you mean." Harlan drew in a deep painful breath, remembered sliding the memory stick out of his pocket and placing it on the bed, remembered the smell of Gina's hair as she leaned over him and picked it up.

"She has it, doesn't she?" insisted Gray Suit, hitting him in the face this time. Harlan felt his nose give and crunch, then a warm flow of blood trailed over his lip and mouth. It was probably broken again. He didn't answer.

"Where are they, Jeffries?" The next blow had him on the ground once more. Blue Suit held up his hand for Gray to stop.

"I told you," Harlan wheezed. "She flipped about the news story. Figured you guys didn't have her best interests at heart. She took the car and left."

"Why didn't you stop her?"

"She had my gun. She…" He laughed at the irony, then spit some blood on the carpet with a silent apology to Shaun. "She put Vicodin in my coffee. Knocked me on my ass. I woke up about five minutes before you got here."

Out the window, he spied a lawn service truck that had pulled up across the street. Two men were wrestling a lawnmower out of the back.

"I don't know where she is." His voice sounded strained to his own ears. His face was bleeding. Gray Suit had a wicked right hook. Harlan said a prayer of gratitude that he'd erased those numbers from the phone. He might have a chance of finding her before they did. If he got away. If they let him live.

Gray Suit took off his jacket, and Blue lifted Harlan to his feet. Gray gave another punch to his kidneys, but Harlan was ready for it and gave with the hit as he rolled. He was much closer to the window now.

"Where's the study? She has it, doesn't she?" Gray Suit said as he stood over him. The man wasn't even breathing hard.

It took Harlan a full minute to catch his breath. Blood

streamed on the carpet from his nose. He could hear the rumbling of a garbage truck in the distance, a lawnmower starting up. "I don't know what you're talking about."

"Sure you do. But I don't think you have it. I think the woman does. We'll find her, and we'll find the study," said Gray Suit.

The truck was getting louder. Blue Suit came forward, pulling a silenced gun from his holster, as some hip-hop tune jangled in his pants pocket. The ring tone combined with the rumbling garbage truck distracted him long enough for Harlan to roll across the floor. Now at the window sill, he crouched and pushed off, diving through the six-foot pane of glass like an Olympic medallist.

Safety glass shattered like spun sugar, and the curtains tangled in the bushes as he burst over the threshold. When he hit the soft turf of the lawn, he clawed the curtains from his face and kept rolling, hearing the soft spit of a silenced gunshot hit behind him.

Filmy fabric streamed behind him as he scrambled to his feet. Holding his side, he half ran, half crawled for the garbage truck in front of the house, shouting at the top of his lungs in order to be heard over the mowers, "Call 9-1-1! Someone's trying to shoot me!"

Another silenced shot struck the pavement behind him. Then another smashed into the garbage hopper, scattering bystanders on the sidewalk.

Harlan could smell the sickly sweet scent of garbage. He climbed aboard the back of the truck, sliding a hand through a strap by the scoop as the driver sped off down the street. Adrenaline kept everything from hurting.

His knee was working, and that was the only thing he could determine at this point. That, and the fact that his nose was still bleeding. Thank God for safety glass or he'd have been history.

At the edge of the neighborhood, the truck ran the stop sign, finally slowing at a busy intersection to stop at a light. Harlan hopped off. He wasn't sure if the workers even knew he'd hitched a ride, but he wasn't taking chances. Getting out of the area as quickly and anonymously as possible seemed the wisest course.

Sirens blared in the distance as he sat at a bus stop several blocks from Shaun's house. Brushing away the bits of glass still clinging to his clothes and hair, he caught a glimpse of his face in the Plexiglas wall around the bus stop enclosure. His cheek and nose were a mess. Grateful his T-shirt was black, he used the sleeve to wipe away the blood.

He tried straightening his hair and dusting off his clothes, but he really needed another baseball cap. Sunglasses, too. The roll across the lawn combined with serving as a punching bag and bursting through the wall yesterday had done a number on his clothes. He looked homeless.

A city bus lumbered to a halt at the stop as a police cruiser raced by in full regalia. Harlan climbed aboard the bus and made his way to the back, fervently hoping the ensuing chaos at Shaun's would keep things busy long enough for him to get a head start on locating Gina.

He hunched down in a seat and tried to figure out what the hell had just happened. Why had Jordan ordered him killed? He reached into his pocket for his cell phone and the piece of paper with the phone numbers he'd found on the handset in Gina's room.

He tried Gina's cell first. As suspected, she didn't answer. He got her voice mail.

"Gina, it's Harlan. Jordan knows you have Shaun's car and it's got a GPS locator service on it. Get away from the Hummer. Take Adam and get away from it. They're looking for you. Let me help. Call me."

He left his number and hung up. Protesting about not being involved wouldn't do him any good at this point. She'd already made up her mind about that.

He stared at the numbers on the paper. She'd called a women's crisis center. Could she have gotten into a safe house with Adam? With her black eye she could have made a story convincing.

He knew he wouldn't get anything if he called the crisis center looking specifically for her. He was going to have to do some fast talking and improvisation. He dialed the number.

"Fairfax County Women's Crisis Center."

"Yes, I'm trying to get some information for a friend of mine." He lowered his voice. "I think…I think her husband is hurting her. She has two young kids. I'm trying to get them out of there. Can you tell me how to get them to a safe place?"

"Could they come stay with you?"

"This is the first place he'd come looking," Harlan confided. "He's a very suspicious man, but there's really nothing he needs to worry about. I'm just her friend, nothing more. Do you have a place she could go?"

"Sir, we can't really give that kind of information out to you. Your friend would have to be the one to contact us. Then we'd set up a place to meet her and go from there."

"I see." Harlan groped for a story. "Could I be the go-between for them? Her husband doesn't…he doesn't let her answer the phone or anything. He's a vicious man."

The woman at the other end of the line cleared her throat.

"I'm sorry, sir. We really can't do that. It's more for safety's sake than anything. Your friend must be the one to make initial contact."

Just what he'd suspected. "Well, I'll talk to her and try to convince her to make the call." He hung up and dialed the second number on his paper.

A woman answered on the third ring. "This is Sheila."

"Sheila, my name is Harlan. I'm Gina's friend." He stopped. The woman didn't fill the silence. "The redhead with the little boy you helped earlier today. They're in trouble."

"Gina? I don't know any Gina. I can't help you."

"She may have given you another name." He was doing this wrong, he could tell.

"I can't talk with you. I'm—"

"Please, I'm not going to ask you where they are. Just give her a message." He waited a moment. "Please, it's very important."

Sheila didn't say anything, so he kept talking. "Tell her that

Jordan will find her car soon. It has a GPS system. She and Adam need to get away from the Hummer so he can't find her. Please call and tell her now."

There was another short beat of silence. "All right. I will."

"Sheila, I want to help her. Ask her to call me." He rattled off the number but didn't get the impression she was writing it down. "I'm not the one who wants to hurt her. Please tell her that."

"I will." There was exasperation and a bit of panic in the woman's voice. "Now will you hang up so I can call her?"

"Sheila?"

"What?"

"Call me back."

Dead air was his answer. Closing the phone, he leaned his head against the top of the bus seat. He knee was trashed, and his back was in knots. The anesthetic effects of his earlier adrenaline rush were gone.

But he felt a tiny ray of hope.

Sheila would call him back. He knew it. She had to.

Chapter Nineteen

Gina chopped fresh fruit and watched the five o'clock news on Channel 8, dreading yet anxious to see if there was any more news about herself and Adam or the Vaccine Safety hearings. Adam colored, while Martin hovered at her feet, hoping for scraps as she worked.

The commentators led off with a story on the president's travels to South America that day. Then Jessica Johns was reporting from a rally on the mall.

"Sandra Hall broke ranks with her party today, and Channel 8 was there for an exclusive look at this maverick senator."

The camera closed in on an older woman with close-cropped hair and an intelligent face. "I'm all for groundbreaking medicines, but they must be safe. To give any company blanket immunity for products it has not yet produced seems the height of irresponsibility to the American public. Shortcuts and blanket vaccine immunity waivers smack of irresponsibility. PharmaVax has over thirty vaccines in their Research and Development pipeline."

Gina stopped chopping fruit and watched, mesmerized as scenes from the autism rally played on-screen. Could this be someone who could help her? If there was any way to meet with the senator, she needed to figure out how to make it happen.

Picking up the house phone, she dialed for directory assistance. Perhaps this woman could take Sarah's study and do something with it. Maybe this was Gina's chance to get the information out in the open—for her and Adam to finally be safe. Two minutes later she had the number.

"Senator Sandra Hall's office."

"Hello, would it be possible for me to get a message to Senator Hall? It's about the Vaccine Safety hearings."

"May I ask who is calling?"

"My name is—" Gina hesitated. "My name's not important. I have some information that the senator needs."

"Perhaps if you could tell me, I could get it to the senator." The staff member was obviously getting ticked off.

"Well, I have a study that I think might be helpful to the debate."

"Can you tell me exactly what the information is?"

"Actually, no. It's for the senator's eyes only."

"I'm sorry, perhaps you could mail it."

Gina ground her teeth together. "Look, I have some very valuable information for the senator that has to do with the vaccine liability waiver issue. I believe this information has a bit of an expiration date. If I mail it, by the time it winds through your mail system and lands on her desk, the hearings will be over."

"Hang on, please, ma'am."

Another voice came on the line. "Ma'am, could you give me your name and address?"

"No, I can't."

"Excuse me. Are you wasting our time?"

"No, it's just…" Gina trailed off and took a deep breath. She wasn't going to get anywhere this way. "My name is Gina Rodgers."

"Okay." This new voice was perky, a woman who sounded like a cheerleader and set Gina's teeth on edge. "Is that Rodgers with a *D*?"

"Right." Hell, this person was an idiot. "Look, try searching my name on Google. You'll get some hits. G-I-N-A R-O-D-G-E-R-S. Throw in Harlan Jeffries, too." Gina rattled off the safe house number and her cell, too. "If Senator Hall wants to talk to me, please have her call me today."

She hung up the phone and took a gulp of Diet Coke, hoping she hadn't just done the worst possible thing for herself and Adam.

The house phone rang immediately. It couldn't be the senator's office that fast. She checked caller ID.

Sheila. The woman didn't waste time on niceties. "I just got a call from a friend of yours, a man named Harlan."

Gina's fingers tightened on the telephone. "What? How did he get your number?"

"I don't know. I'm not sure that's important right now."

"What did he say?"

"Your car has a GPS locator, and someone named Jordan has the code. Harlan said to get away from the car."

Gina's world tilted.

"He wants you to call him, Gina."

She didn't say anything. Sheila had just called her Gina. "You know my name."

"I don't care what your real name is, honey. It doesn't matter to me. If a woman is in trouble, she's in trouble.

"He says he doesn't want to hurt you. That he was never the one who hurt you. Is that true?"

She squeezed her eyes shut and gripped the phone. Everything was unraveling. "Yes, it's true." She knew it was.

"Who is Jordan?"

"I can't tell you." *It's coming too fast.* "I don't know that you'd believe me. He's very dangerous."

She looked out the window at the big blue Hummer parked in the driveway. She imagined it even now guiding men who wanted to hurt her and Adam to their doorstep.

"What are you gonna do, Gina?"

She didn't answer. She was too busy thinking. Had Harlan been in on this all along?

No. If he was in on it, why even call and tell her they had a way of finding her? They could just show up and have her. She'd never be the wiser.

God, she was going to have to go with her gut, which was

scarier than anything that had happened today. She would have to trust herself.

In her heart she knew there was no way Harlan was working for PharmaVax. If he was, he'd never have let her see the study he'd printed at Kinko's. He hadn't known the study was even in their possession until Gina found the memory stick inside Dickens.

But Harlan was working for Jordan, and something was very wrong there. Could she trust Harlan with the study? She had no idea. The only thing she was sure of was that Harlan wouldn't hurt Adam. He'd already had too many opportunities to do that.

He could have killed them both at the lake house or even at Shaun's before she'd overdosed him on his painkillers. Lord knows he'd had every opportunity to get close enough last night. He'd had the study then, and later she'd been…very willing.

"Sheila, do you have his number?"

"Yes, he asked me to call him back after I talked to you."

She closed her eyes again and took a deep breath. This was it. Crunch time.

Gina opened her eyes and took another deep breath. "Okay. I want you to call him and get him out here."

"Are you sure?"

"No, I'm not. It's crazy. But I'm out of sane ideas here." She quit staring and started across the kitchen to the bedroom, gathering their things as she went. "I'm taking Adam, and we're leaving."

"Leaving? Where will you go? It's nothing but woods and farmland around there."

"I know. We're going hiking. I can't do that by myself with an autistic five-year-old and men with guns after me. Tell Harlan I'm counting on his being able to find us before they do. I'll try calling him once we're away from the house and safe."

"But the cell signal…"

"I know, it's lousy." Gina stopped for a moment. "Tell him he'll have to track me."

"Are you sure?"

"Sheila, I'm not sure about anything. But I'm completely out of options here. We can't tromp around in the woods for long and not get caught."

"I can call the police."

"Some of these people *were* the police in Mississippi. I don't know that it's any different here."

"Be careful."

"You, too. I don't know how far this thing reaches. I'm sorry I lied to you about needing help." Gina found her purse and shoved her recharged cell phone inside.

"You didn't lie. You are in trouble, and men are trying to kill you. You just don't fit our usual profile."

Gina huffed a laugh. "Well, it's good to know I'm an original. Thank you for helping me and Adam." She hung up and raced to gather the boy and Martin for their trek into the woods. By trusting her instincts, she was trusting Harlan. She hoped she wasn't making the biggest mistake of her life.

HARLAN LEANED BACK in the seat. His knee throbbed, and his back was spasming more than it had in months. But none of that mattered. Gina trusted him, or she'd decided he was the devil she knew. Either way, he would be in a position to help her. "Where are we going?" he asked.

"To Ka—I mean Gina." Sheila gave him a sideways glance. "She and Adam are about an hour from here, in Maryland. It's in the middle of nowhere. She doesn't have a cell signal. You're going to have to find her and the boy in the woods once you get there. She's left the farmhouse where the car was parked."

He raised an eyebrow. "What, no flaming hoops or anything?"

"No." Sheila didn't crack a smile. She hadn't spoken much since she'd picked him up at the bus stop in Tysons Corner. She'd taken one look at his battered face and handed him a first aid kit from behind her seat along with a bottle of water.

"Do you need anything else?" she asked.

"Flashlight, water and, uh…you got any aspirin in this box?"

She shot him another sideways glance. "Help yourself."

He dug around and found the bottle of painkillers.

"Have you eaten anything?" Sheila was eyeing him again as she navigated the road. "Open the glove box. I've got some energy bars in there. You're going to need something."

He did as he was told and ate three of the protein bars, afterward leaning his head back against the seat. If he could close his eyes for ten minutes, he'd be good to go. He woke as Sheila pulled off the highway into a gas station. She handed him the keys and got out of the car.

"You're sure you want to go through with this?" she asked as he slid into the driver's seat. "I could wait for you here."

"No." Harlan turned to face her, hoping to drive his point home. "Get a cab back to the city. Wait until tomorrow and report the car stolen."

"I won't do that."

"Sheila, if you don't hear from us, you have to. I don't know how this is going to look tomorrow. If it doesn't go our way, reporting this car stolen is the only chance to prove you weren't involved."

She nodded imperceptibly, but he could tell she wasn't going to do it. Mentally he forced himself to shrug. He couldn't save everybody, no matter how he tried. "Tell me about the property this house sits on."

"It's about thirty acres. Mostly timber. A river runs through the center of it." She used her hands to gesture. "It's bounded on two sides by the highway—one side by a large hill, and the other opens onto the adjoining property. That's about four hundred acres of timber."

"Okay, so we're talking about a significant area to search. If they think she's taken to the woods, that's actually good." He looked at her. "Why are you doing this?"

She didn't hesitate. "Because someone stuck her neck out for me once when I needed help."

He didn't know what to say besides the obvious. Even that seemed inadequate. "Thank you."

"Be careful. Call me if I can help."

"Help us by getting a cab back to town."

He pulled out of the station and followed the map she'd drawn.

Chapter Twenty

The sun was low in the sky when Harlan found the place Sheila had indicated on her hastily drawn map. He passed the house about two hundred yards back from the tree-lined gravel road and turned around to cruise by again.

He parked on the shoulder of the main road, just a lost passerby getting his bearings. Two cars were in the drive. One was a Hummer, and the other looked like the sedan from earlier today at Shaun's. Blue Suit and Gray Suit had beaten him out here.

He pulled up a quarter of a mile and parked, so his car couldn't be seen from the house. Stepping out of the Volvo, he shouldered the backpack and slogged through a shallow ditch. When he walked into the trees, he was immediately engulfed in quiet.

All he could hear were the sounds of the forest—birds twittering, wind blowing through the new spring foliage. He took out his cell phone, hoping for a signal of some sort.

Nothing.

Hell, that would have been too easy.

He began the hike in, heading straight for the middle of the woods.

GINA ARRIVED AT THE run-down cabin and sank to her knees on the broken porch. She'd carried the dog and Adam halfway there. Adam scrambled off her back and dashed to the water's edge with Martin.

Panting and out of breath, Gina let them go for just a minute. She couldn't move to get them if she had to. They'd waded through the shallow river—it was more of a stream—maybe three feet deep. That, combined with the hills, had done her in. She had no idea if anyone was back at the house yet, but just the fact that the men who had killed Tammy and Sarah could find the car frightened her.

Adam was fussing. He hadn't wanted to leave the cozy farmhouse. She didn't blame him. She hadn't wanted to leave either.

Martin was limping. He'd stepped into a bramble patch and that's how she'd ended up carrying him under one arm while Adam rode piggyback.

The phone in her bag began its island ring tone, signaling a return of service. She scrambled to dig through her bag and turn the ringer to Vibrate as she answered.

She noted the D.C. area code but didn't recognize the number. When she flipped open the headset, no one was there. She hit End. Because the signal strength was mediocre, she tried texting Harlan. She'd left a trail a blind elephant could follow, but it never hurt to let him know where she was while she had the means to do so.

TEN MINUTES INTO the woods Harlan's knee was throbbing, which pretty much took his mind off his hurting back. As he crested the top of a small hill, he pulled out the cell phone again. Amazingly, he now had a signal and a text message.

Near the river. Old shack. South. I think.

He texted back, walking at the same time.

On my way. Stay out of sight. Stay put.

His knee protested as he moved silently across the hilly terrain. According to Sheila, a river ran through the center of the property. Hopefully, he didn't have that far to limp. The trick was going to be finding that shack before Jordan's people did.

That's how he thought of them now. And he still couldn't believe it. The man he'd trusted, looked up to and loved like a father had used him and been ready to kill him when his usefulness was done.

He shook his head and concentrated on listening for sounds that didn't belong here in the forested area. Twigs snapping underfoot. The rasp of fabric brushing up against a tree trunk. Anything out of place.

He took a moment and stood very still.

He couldn't hear anything out of the ordinary. The woods muffled everything too well. He focused on making sure he was moving quietly enough not to be heard by anyone else who was out looking for Gina and Adam. Twenty minutes later he picked up a trail. He couldn't tell if it was Gina or Jordan's men, but it was his best option.

His phone vibrated at his hip. Another message.

I hear noise That U?

He stopped to type back.

No B still B quiet.

He hurried on through the woods, past dead logs and over trampled grass from the person or persons who had passed before him. Where was the shack? He had to be getting close. He was at the top of another rise when he heard it.

A small *snick*.

He froze. He knew that particular noise, the sound a gun makes when ammunition is sliding into the chamber. He hit the ground and rolled as several shots rang out, striking the tree and ground beside him.

Bark flew in the air, peppering his forehead. Gunshots still echoed through the woods as he rolled down a small hill and came to a hard stop against a large fallen tree. Disoriented from his dizzying ride down the embankment, he lay there trying to figure out which end was up and how to catch his breath.

He took inventory. His forehead was the only thing bleeding. No broken bones. But no gun either. Hell, he didn't even have a big stick. He could hear his assailant crashing through the underbrush down the hill. He had maybe two minutes before the guy would be on top of him.

Harlan felt a puff of air on his face and really looked at the log he was resting against. It was hollow with a split down the side. A breeze was coming off the water through the slit from the other side. He heard the stream gurgling. Felt the dead leaves all around him from the tree's branches.

What were his options?

With his knee, he couldn't run fast enough at this point.

He could try brushing some of the leaves on top of himself. Camouflaging that way would work, but there were hardly enough leaves to do the job, and he would make too much racket in the process.

He crawled to the end of the stump, brushing a few leaves behind him as he went in an effort to cover the largest of his tracks. Huge roots stuck out of the bottom of the fallen tree like spikes, hanging down into the water at the stream's edge. But inside the trunk was completely hollow. In the brush he heard footsteps drawing closer, allowing him no choice.

Shoving his way past clammy dead roots, he ignored the slimy feel of the mold and the crawling bugs whose home he was disturbing and slid inside the trunk.

He had a clear view of the path he'd taken down the hill through the slit that ran the entire length of the log. He'd just shimmied all the way inside when blue pant legs came into view. Harlan could see the tracks he'd made as he'd crawled around by the river. It looked as though an army had walked around the tree trunk. But his would-be assailant seemed oblivious and kept right on walking.

Then he heard Gina's voice.

"Adam, Adam, come back."

His heart sank.

"Adam, no."

Chapter Twenty-One

Gina and Adam huddled in a filthy corner of the ramshackle shack. Shots rang out, audible even over the sound of rushing water. Holding tightly to the boy and crouched beside a rusted-out cot, she peered out a broken window as Harlan burst into view and crashed into a dead tree at the river's edge.

"Harlan! Harlan!" cried Adam.

"Shh. I know, baby, I know." Gina tightened her grip on his arm. "We've got to wait here, honey."

She knew Adam couldn't stand to be restrained, but there was no way she was letting him outside. She didn't know what was going on yet.

Adam squirmed and wriggled, then Martin began to growl, low in the back of his throat. She looked through jagged glass to the top of the hill. Someone else was up there and on the way down.

From here it looked to be a man, a big man. He was holding a rifle and headed straight toward Harlan and the tree.

Thankfully, he hadn't seen Harlan yet. Gina held her breath as Harlan made his way around the massive trunk and disappeared inside. She thought through her limited options. Harlan's gun was in her bag, on the other side of the cabin.

Martin continued to growl. Adam wriggled and squirmed, then bent down and bit her hand. She was so surprised, she let go.

Adam broke free and raced for the door.

"Adam, Adam, come back." She watched as he made a beeline for Harlan. The man in blue looked up in surprise.

"Adam, no." She dove for her bag and raced after the boy.

When she got out on the porch, the man was snatching Adam up as he tore by on his way to the tree. She sidestepped the rotting floorboards and ripped the gun from her purse, thankful she'd left the ammunition in the clip. Harlan would have had a fit if he'd known she'd been carrying a loaded handgun in her purse while she had Adam with her.

Adam began to shriek, his feet dangling off the ground.

"Hey!" she shouted. "Let him go." She pointed the gun, but her hands were shaking badly. The man just looked at her as he dropped the rifle and pulled a knife from his pocket. The late afternoon sun reflected off the jagged blade he pressed to Adam's side.

"No!" she screamed. *This could not be happening.*

Completely unaware of the danger, Adam howled his frustration again at being held so tightly. He squirmed, then bent his head and clamped down on the man's hand with his teeth.

The man jerked his hand aside, and Adam wriggled away. He started forward with the knife. Gina fired at him and screamed again when Adam slid to the ground at his feet.

She watched the man, a look of complete bafflement on his face. His expression didn't change as he crumpled like a newspaper and fell face forward into the water.

Shocked, she stared in utter silence, not believing she had shot a man.

ADAM HOWLED AT THE top of his lungs. Harlan couldn't see anything from inside the tree trunk, and he couldn't hear Gina. He began clawing his way out. He heard scurrying and scuffling noises, but he couldn't decipher their meaning. Frustrated and helpless, he was out seconds later, dreading what he would find. Knowing it would be like his nightmares all over again.

Splashing through knee-deep water, he couldn't quite trust his own eyes. Gina was standing over Blue Suit, holding the Glock she'd pointed at him in Shaun's kitchen earlier that morning. Her eyes were wide with shock. She was trembling, and her hair looked like she'd hacked it off with a pair of garden shears.

She was staring at the man and the six-inch hunting knife still gripped in his hand. Behind her Adam was sprawled on the ground clutching Dickens to his chest. Tears streamed down the boy's cheeks as Martin licked his face.

Blue Suit was dead or giving a fair impression of it. She'd gotten him in the head. It wasn't pretty, but it was effective.

Harlan felt a bug crawling on his neck and reached up to brush it off. The movement caught her attention where his splashing hadn't. She lifted the gun and pointed it at him.

"Gina?"

Adam lifted his head at Harlan's voice. "Harlan," he whispered. More tears ran down his cheeks.

"Gina, it's me." Harlan raised his hands to his side. "Put the gun down, okay?"

She tightened her hands on the Glock.

"It's me. Harlan. I know you're pissed, but I don't think you want to shoot me." He kept his tone smooth and steady. "Gina?"

She seemed to realize what she was doing and suddenly exhaled, lowering the gun. "Harlan? Harlan, oh, God." She dropped the Glock and sank to the ground. "Oh, Jesus. I can't believe I did that.

"He was coming for me and for Adam, and he had a hold of him and had that knife, and I just… Oh my God, I shot him. I can't believe I did that." She was babbling and crying and shaking her head.

Harlan went to her then and held her, gathering her in his arms. He didn't tell her it was okay, because it was far from okay.

But he did say, "You did the right thing. You and Adam are safe now." He felt her trembling against his chest, struggling to catch her breath. It would be so easy to stay like this for too long.

He gave her arms a squeeze and pushed her away. "Gina, we have to leave, right now." He bent down and picked up his Glock.

"There's someone else here looking for you. He had to have heard those shots. We've got to get out of here."

He bent down to Adam and helped him up. "Come on, big guy. Let's 'move it, move it.'" He imitated Adam's favorite character from *Madagascar*. Normally that would have gotten at least a giggle, but the boy barely looked up.

"Come on." He took Adam's hand and started back up the riverbank.

They had to get out of the area before Gray Suit came looking for his buddy. This was one thing he could help Gina do. She seemed to have taken care of everything else.

Suddenly, he was inexplicably angry and had to fight to keep his tone even. "We'll go upstream a way, then go back out toward the road."

Gina was still staring at Blue Suit.

"Come on, Gina. Now!" He sharpened his voice. They had to move.

She looked at him with horror in her eyes. "What have I done?"

He sighed, biting back the first words that came to mind. *What you've wanted to do all along. You saved yourself.* He recognized the fact, even if she didn't.

He couldn't blame her for his anger. It wasn't her fault that her competence made him mad. It was the feeling of helplessness that had him tied in knots.

He softened the words. "He was here to kill you and Adam. You just saved your own lives."

GINA SLOGGED UP THE riverbank, struggling to rush through the mud behind Harlan and Adam. She still couldn't comprehend what had just happened.

She'd shot and killed a man. He'd been about to kill her nephew, but still… Was there a way she could have done something different to—

She tripped, bumping into Harlan's chest. He had to grab her wrist to keep her from falling.

"Gina, stop thinking about it. We've got to get out of here. Remember, 'doing what's necessary.' That's what you did. And I know you're capable of holding it together until we're out of here and safe."

His face was anything but sympathetic. "Adam's keeping up better than you are right now. So hang on. There'll be time to think it through and 'what if' yourself to death later. For now, move."

His voice was harsh. The words stung. But he was right. She'd better suck it up or shooting that guy would be for nothing if someone else found them. She nodded and headed uphill again, this time at a much faster clip.

She tried not to think about the fact that she'd shot someone. But with every step, it seemed to reverberate through her brain. She was a murderer...a killer.

She jogged after Adam and Harlan. The boy's jeans were torn at the calf from their trek through the woods. God, how was she going to help him? How was she going to keep him if she went to prison?

Dr. Phillips would say she was projecting her fears into the future and all other kinds of psycho babble. She was way past *screwup*. Her shrink on speed dial wasn't going to be any help at all with this unless he knew a good lawyer. She choked back the hysteria bubbling up and kept jogging.

Up ahead Harlan stopped. There was a sharp "pftt" sound, and bark flew inches from her head.

"Get down! Get down!" Harlan shouted as he leaned back to push her head to the ground.

She hit the dirt and tried to pull Adam with her, but the boy was having none of it. He'd had enough. He jerked back against her hand and wrenched his fingers from her grasp. Still standing, he backed away and began to run in the opposite direction from both her and Harlan, carrying Dickens under his arm.

"No!" Gina shouted.

Harlan took off after him amid more flying bark. Martin ran

after them both, yapping like mad, leaving Gina alone in the eerily quiet woods. She lay in the dirt, in shock.

She could smell the damp earth and feel the soft breeze. In the distance she heard the dog bark and catapulted into action, racing toward the sound. There was shouting and scrambling in the underbrush—and Adam, screaming.

She ran until her side had a stitch in it. She walked, then ran again. She heard someone else running in front of her and hoped it was Harlan, but she didn't shout out for fear it wasn't.

She heard Adam crying. Martin furiously barking. A yelp. Then nothing.

Finally, she reached the edge of the trees. An arm snaked out and grabbed her just as she was about to step out of the cover of the woods.

She stifled a gasp.

It was Harlan, visibly upset, the lines around his mouth rigid with anger. He held her tightly to his side with Dickens and Martin under his other arm. He leaned into her ear. "They have Adam and several reinforcements."

He nodded toward the driveway. There were two cars in addition to the dark sedan and Shaun's Hummer. Four men—two with rifles—stood by the hood.

Gray Suit carried Adam. The boy was struggling but tired and very much overpowered.

"Oh my God. What are they doing with him?"

"They're waiting for us."

"To do what?" Gina whispered, straining against his arm, desperate to move forward. Harlan held her fast, clamping her to him with one arm.

"Exactly what you're doing."

"Let go of me!" She pushed against him as the men shoved Adam into one of the cars and slammed the door.

One by one the cars drove toward the highway, no more than thirty feet from where Gina and Harlan hid in the trees. She moved to step forward again, and Harlan's arm tightened even more.

"Don't," he warned.

Gina felt her frustration change into something ugly and desperate. "Do something," she hissed.

"What do you want me to do?" He cast eyes on her that were black in their ferocity. "I have a dust-mop dog, exactly four bullets and you. What can I do that won't get us killed or captured?"

Frantic to hold on to something that had been next to Adam, she reached for the stuffed animal tucked under Harlan's arm and pulled it to her, focusing on the lime-green stitches she'd emblazoned across Dickens's chest. "What's going to happen?" she whispered, unable to watch as the cars drove out of sight.

"They'll want to make a trade."

"How do you know that?" She glanced up, but Harlan's eyes never left the road.

He shrugged. "Because we've got what they want. And they've got what we want."

"The study?"

He nodded. "You have it with you?"

"Yes." She patted her jeans pocket. "What do we do?"

He finally looked down at her, his eyes mirroring her own anger and frustration. "We wait."

Chapter Twenty-Two

Fifteen minutes later they were hurtling down the highway in Sheila's Volvo. Gina's shirt was damp with perspiration, and her heart was numb with fear and frustration.

"Where are we going?" she asked.

Harlan's hands were white-knuckled on the steering wheel. "I have no idea. You got any suggestions?"

She shook her head. "I haven't a clue." She looked out the window at the passing countryside—the wooded hills and occasional pasture. "I suppose our pictures are all over the news here, as well."

"If they're not, they will be soon. Jordan will see to that. The Amber Alert is probably nationwide by now."

Her cell phone vibrated in her pocket. Apparently, the signal strength was working just fine out here. She dug the phone out of her jeans. She didn't recognize the number, but it was a D.C. area code.

"Hello?"

"Gina Rodgers?"

She switched the phone to Speaker. "Yes, this is she."

"I believe I have something of yours." It was a woman's voice. Low and husky.

Gina thought she could hear Adam crying in the background. "Is he all right?" She strained to listen. Yes, she was sure it was

Adam. He was wailing. She'd never been so glad to hear Adam cry. He had to be working himself into a state without Harlan, Martin or Dickens there. He'd probably even settle for Gina at this point.

"The boy is fine, and he'll remain that way. I believe you have some information for me."

She looked at Harlan. He was staring straight ahead. "You mean my sister's study? Yes, I have it."

"I propose a trade." The voice was detached. Cool.

Harlan nodded grimly.

"All right. How do we do this?"

"Come to the senator's house. We'll trade there."

"How do we—?"

"Your man can get you there."

"My man—?"

"Let me talk to the soldier."

"What?"

"Let me talk to the man with you and take it off speakerphone." The voice had grown impatient.

Gina switched off the speaker and handed the phone to Harlan.

"This is Jeffries." Gina listened and watched his eyes harden. "No, it wasn't. I'm sorry. I would have rather been the one." His voice was cold, colder than the woman's on the phone. She'd never heard this tone before. "I'll look forward to it."

He clicked the phone shut. "All right, it's done. We've got a place to meet." He pressed down on the accelerator. "We've got some shopping to do before we get—"

The ringing phone interrupted him. He gazed ferociously at it with a look in his eyes Gina had never seen until tonight. Only after he studied the caller ID did he calmly hand the cell to her. "This isn't the same number."

"Hello?"

"I'm trying to reach Gina Rodgers." This was a different woman. Her voice was brisk and businesslike but much warmer and somewhat familiar.

"This is she."

"My name is Senator Sandra Hall. I understand you've been trying to reach me."

Gina swallowed. "Yes, yes, I have."

Harlan looked at her. "Who is it?" he mouthed.

Gina clicked on the speakerphone. "Why?" the senator asked.

"Are you tracing this call, Senator Hall?"

"Should I be?"

"Well, I think you know who I am, so I'd be surprised if you weren't."

Senator Hall didn't answer. Harlan motioned for Gina to go ahead. She spoke quickly.

"I have some information about vaccine safety and—" She stopped and looked at Harlan. His mouth was a thin, harsh line. But he nodded. "And about Jordan Bell that I think can help you with the vaccine liability waiver issue."

"I'd like to talk with you," said the senator.

"I can meet you, but not until later. I've got something to take care of first."

She wouldn't tell Sandra Hall about Adam but agreed to call her back in a few hours. The situation was too dangerous until they had the child back. But she did decide to mail her the copy of Sarah's study. It was the very least Gina could do, in case this all went sideways tonight.

LIGHTS BLAZED FROM the crystal-paned windows of Jordan's two-story Tudor estate. The house was lit for a party. Multiple cars lined the circular drive as Harlan and Gina pulled up. The night felt surreal. If he closed his eyes, Harlan could almost imagine it was a holiday spent with Jimmy and his dad. Or the wedding two years ago. Or the funeral less than six months ago.

Of course, that day the mansion hadn't been lit up for a party. It had been a blistering hot summer afternoon, and he'd been transported in an ambulance to attend the service. He scrubbed his face with his hands to clear the memories and turned off the ignition.

Gina sat beside him. She'd been growing quieter since their stops at Target and the electronics store. He'd asked her to call Senator Hall back. She hadn't wanted to, but he'd insisted.

Thunder rolled as they walked up the front steps. Taylor, the butler he'd known half his life, opened the door. The old man's eyes widened when he recognized Harlan, but he recovered quickly and welcomed him inside.

"Taylor, this is Miss Rodgers."

The older man inclined his head and left them in the foyer to find his employer or go call the police. Harlan wasn't sure which. He could hear voices and laughter coming from the living room toward the back of the house. There was a party going on, no doubt celebrating the passage of PharmaVax's vaccine liability waiver. He and Gina had heard the news on the way here. The bill had passed in Congress an hour ago.

Moments later Jordan appeared, looking as if he'd just stepped out of a J. Crew catalog. He held a glass of champagne in one hand. His smooth look was at odds with his baffled expression. "Harlan? What are you doing here?"

Harlan tried to ignore the spurt of anger that bubbled up inside his chest. If he gave in to it, he might erupt. "We got a phone call that told us to come here for the trade."

"Trade?" Jordan was all confusion, looking from one to the other—taking in Harlan's battered face and Gina's black eye and torn clothes. "What happened to you?"

"What didn't? You tried to kill us, remember? They took the boy. What the hell is going on? I thought you were supposed to be all concerned with the results of Sarah Sutton's study, not giving out liability waivers like free candy."

Jordan didn't react. On the surface, at least, he remained the master politician. "That's not true. Things are not how they appear. Really, it's much more complicat—"

"Don't even begin to try to bullshit me. I don't care. We just want Adam." Anger fizzed in his bloodstream like the bubbles in Jordan's champagne. "Remember, I've had people shoot at me over the past four days, and now I've seen the trail of bodies. Where's Adam?"

A crack appeared in the senator's demeanor. "I don't know where the boy is. I'm afraid I don't know what's happening here tonight. Come into the study, and we'll talk. This may take a while."

Taylor returned to the entryway with two other men. Security, but not secret service. Harlan walked past without making eye contact.

"You're very brave coming here if you think I'm trying to kill you." Jordan put down the champagne on his desk and poured himself a scotch. "Or foolish." Harlan shook his head when Jordan held up the bottle to offer him a drink as well. The older man shrugged and tossed back the liquor. "Which is it?"

"Probably a little of both. But you're holding all the cards, and we want the boy back. Besides, I figure with all these people, you wouldn't risk it. The bill's been voted in. Why would you care anymore? We'll give you the study. We just want Adam."

Jordan's face took on a shrewd look. "You have it with you?"

"Yes. They told us to come here to make the trade. The study for the boy. We're here to do that. Who called us?"

"I did." A woman stepped into the room. Dressed in designer attire, she looked to be mid-forties, distinctive.

Jordan visibly paled. "Why would you do that?"

"I…we have our reasons," she murmured, striding into the room as if she lived there.

"Who are you?" asked Gina.

"No one of consequence, Miss Rodgers, I assure you. Call me Marnie. But you, my dear, you are very important. I believe you have something that I need."

"Why?" asked Harlan. "The bill will be law in a matter of days, once the president signs it."

"Insurance, Mr. Jeffries, insurance. Haven't you heard? Sandra Hall has everyone so stirred up they're talking about a presidential veto."

Gina stepped forward beside Harlan. "But we don't care about any of this. We just want Adam back. Where is he?"

"He's safe. For now. Where's the study?"

"We ha—" Gina began.

Harlan leaned into her, interrupting. "The boy for the study. That's what we agreed to. Then we'll be gone."

The woman nodded. "Yes, yes. That is what was agreed to. Although, I'd venture to guess that you'd be willing to change our bargain if I insisted."

Marnie stared hard at both of them. Weighing them. Studying. "All right." She turned to the security guards. "Miss Rodgers and I are going to get the boy. Senator Bell and Mr. Jeffries are to stay here."

"Harlan?" murmured Gina.

"We don't want to be separated," said Harlan.

"Well, that's very sweet, but I can't parade both of you through the house. There is a rather large party going on in the next room, and you and Ms. Rodgers— May I call you Gina?"

Gina didn't respond.

"Your and Gina's pictures are all over the news. They wouldn't recognize Gina here. She's done quite the job of disguising herself. That haircut. What did you use, honey? Kitchen shears?" Marnie shuddered. "Never mind, don't tell me. But you—" She put a hand on Harlan's arm, "I'm afraid, there is just no disguising you, Mr. Jeffries. You'll have to wait here."

"All right," said Gina. "Please, take me to Adam."

Harlan touched her hand. "Gina—"

Marnie nodded to them both. "It's perfectly fine. I've no interest in harming either of you. I just want the study results, and then I'm out of here. Jordan gives rather dull parties as far as I'm concerned."

"Why are you doing this?" asked Jordan. "Why are you here, tonight of all nights? This could ruin it all."

"Don't fret, Jordan. It's all under control." She patted his cheek like she would a four year-old's. "I told you, dear, it's insurance. The people I work for never want you to think you're more powerful than you are. No matter what office you hold. Pour yourself another drink, honey. You look like you could use one."

She turned to Gina and slipped her arm through her elbow. "I'm just going to tag along with Gina to get little Adam. We'll be right back." She left in a cloud of Chanel, escorting Gina, looking for all the world as if she was giving her a grand tour of the mansion.

Harlan watched them, wondering if there was any way to go after her. He looked at the guards, noted the guns under their jackets and realized going after her was out of the question. Unless he wanted to get shot.

Gina had to be safe in this house full of VIPs for the time being. One scream, and the farce would be over.

He couldn't believe it would be this easy. Things were never this easy. But maybe, just this once…

He studied Jordan. Really looked at him and wondered how he could have been so wrong. How he could have been so mistaken about the man's character. All that time when he was in the hospital and Jordan was coming to see him. J.B. had promised Harlan that he didn't blame him for Jimmy's death.

Jordan poured himself another scotch, seemingly on Marnie's advice and pointed to a chair, motioning for Harlan to sit. "You want something?"

The last thread holding Harlan's temper in check snapped. "I want to know what the hell is going on. I think you owe me that."

Jordan looked up from pouring his drink. Liquor sloshed over the sides of the glass. "Owe you that? Owe you that?" Jordan's voice raised on that last. "My son is dead."

"I know that. I watched him get blown to bits. But I didn't kill him. You hear me? I didn't do it." Harlan gripped the sides of the chair. "A roadside bomb killed him. So quit blaming me. God knows I've blamed myself enough for both of us. It wasn't my fault."

Harlan stopped talking, aghast that he'd said out loud what he'd been thinking for the past six months. It wasn't his fault.

He couldn't save Jimmy. The declaration was freeing, but he didn't have time to focus on everything it meant now.

"Gina Rodgers's sister is dead. So is her friend Tammy. Not to mention Kate Brooks and William Sullivan. I think you know something about all that. What happened?"

At the mention of his son, all the fight seemed to have gone out of Jordan. He opened a hand as he sat across from Harlan. "Where do I start?"

"How about at the beginning, where you send me to Starkville to work with Adam Sutton. Was this all in the works even then?"

Jordan looked at his feet, then back at Harlan. "Yes, some of it was in play then. That's why I sent you. I wanted someone there I knew. Someone I trusted."

"Why?"

"I had been asked to keep an eye on the study. To let them know how it went."

"Who is *them*?"

"PharmaVax." He waved a hand toward the door the women had just walked through. "Marnie."

"Why? Why would you care?" He thought he knew the answer, but he needed to hear Jordan say the words.

"They are a very large contributor to my campaign."

"Is that all they wanted?"

"No, but that's all they asked at first. Just for me to keep an eye on it. That was fairly easy. Sarah was at my alma mater. I got an introduction to her last fall on one of my trips down there for a football game."

Even though he'd known the information was coming, Harlan's reaction surprised him. Furious and devastated at the same time, his hand tightened on the armrest as his heart rate sped up. *Why?*

"PharmaVax said they'd contribute to my presidential campaign if I could keep them abreast of anything happening with the study here in Washington. Anything happening with the study in D.C. seemed fairly unlikely, so I said all right—never dreaming what was to come."

Harlan began wishing he'd taken Jordan up on the scotch. The rain had yet to fall, but the wind blowing outside was brushing a tree limb against one of the windows. The older man's words came faster now.

"PharmaVax wanted a vaccine liability waiver so they could finish manufacturing their H3N6 vaccine. Lawsuits were slowing research and development and the production lines to a crawl. PharmaVax is the closest of all the drug companies in the world to a viable vaccine for a virus with a 95 percent mortality rate. But the legal wrangling with liability lawsuits is about to take them under."

"Was there a reason for all those lawsuits?" asked Harlan. "Were they sloppy? Inept?"

Jordan didn't answer him and wouldn't meet his eyes. Instead he stood and poured himself another drink. Harlan's stomach twisted.

"Sarah's study could have proven quite damaging to their case for blanket liability immunity," Jordan continued, "*if* the study got much publicity. A minor study from a university wouldn't have made much difference. Still, PharmaVax wanted to stop the study from coming to light before the vaccine liability waiver went through."

He took a sip of the drink, and Harlan realized the older man's hands were shaking. This had taken on a nightmarish quality.

"I swear, I only thought they'd break into her lab," said Jordan. "But when they found out about the Daubert hearing, that changed everything. Sullivan's scheduled court date was right on top of our hearings. A case with that kind of publicity in the autism community would have brought forth a whole avalanche of civil lawsuits."

He leaned forward, anxious to make his case to someone who would listen and possibly give absolution. "It would have made the morning talk shows and the evening news cycles for weeks. Blanket liability immunity would have been impossible to get through Congress."

"So they decided to erase the study?"

Jordan's face fell. "That's a horrible way to say it, but yes. I didn't realize for certain that's what was happening until the night Sarah disappeared."

"But you suspected," said Harlan.

"I heard about Sullivan's death but hoped it had been an accident. By the time I knew the truth—" He gripped the glass in both hands. "Well, by then I was too far in. We were already in the middle of the hearings. My God, think of the publicity if my part in this came out. Harlan, you've got to believe me. I never would have done this if I'd known how far they were going to go."

Harlan's disgust and anger welled up, turning into something ugly and black. "You mean you'd prostitute yourself for something small but not go all the way? God, why didn't you stop it? Why didn't you refuse?" *I thought you were better than that.*

Jordan didn't answer.

"Because of a little campaign money?" Harlan shook his head in revulsion. "I don't know you anymore. I'm not sure I ever did. You aren't who I thought you were. You're sure as hell not who Jimmy thought you were."

Jordan seemed to reel for a moment as if he'd been punched in the face. Then he straightened and set the glass back on the table. His hands were steady now, his eyes clear and cold.

"It's more than just a *little* campaign money, Harlan. We're talking *the* campaign. Whatever I need for a full boat ride to the White House."

Harlan shook his head. "Doesn't matter how much or how little they pay you. If you're selling out, you're just negotiating a price. You've already proven you're a whore."

"It's not just the campaign."

He laughed bitterly. "Don't lie, Jordan. I know how much you've always wanted this. It was a running joke with Jimmy."

"But don't you see?" insisted Jordan. "If we take down the pharmaceutical companies with liability lawsuits, what's left for us?"

"What do you mean?"

"I mean, say we get the pharmaceutical companies. We make those guys pay for the damages they've done with the whole autism issue. Hell, it'd bankrupt everyone of 'em. None of them will be manufacturing vaccines or even antibiotics anymore. Then where will we be?

"Forget this pandemic that's coming. Even regular medications for diabetes, cancer, even strep throat are at risk. If the government doesn't get these protections in place and we just let the lawyers have at it, we'll kill the very companies that can save us."

Harlan leaned back and looked him in the eye. Did Jordan really believe this, or was it one more justification for his actions? "But if the pharmaceutical companies and the government both know there's a problem with some of their vaccines, why can't that be acknowledged and fixed instead of going forward like this?"

"Because of the lawsuits, son. The government must have the protections in place before we acknowledge the problems—or we're sunk. And it's not just us. It's every civilized country in the world. Every third world nation we sell a vaccine to could come after us from a legal standpoint on this issue, not to mention our own citizens. Governments and big pharma both would be considered liable. PharmaVax can't handle that kind of liability. And no one wants to sink a company that can stop a pandemic."

"But what about a company that's already caused an epidemic? That's what they're calling it now. Kate Brooks said one out of every one hundred sixty-six children has autism. Sarah Sutton's study proves some of it was most likely caused by the thimerosal additive in vaccines. If that's not an epidemic, what is?"

The older man didn't answer. Harlan stood, no longer willing to even argue the point. It didn't matter, because Harlan had just figured it out. "But you'll be president of the United States, and PharmaVax will have all of their precious vaccines, plus their profits with no liability. So who cares, righ—?"

The doors opened and Gina came in carrying a sleeping Adam. *Save someone you can.* Jimmy's voice echoed in his mind. Gina's expression was tight. She was obviously furious.

Adam's face was grubby except for where a trail of tears had washed his cheeks clean.

Save someone you can. "Is he all right?" asked Harlan.

Gina nodded but didn't speak.

"He's sedated," said Marnie, following at her elbow. "We felt he would be more comfortable this way. He was rather agitated when he got here."

Bitch. No wonder Gina was angry.

Marnie faced him. "Did you and Jordan get to chat? Catch up on family news?"

Harlan winced inwardly at the implication.

Marnie didn't wait for an answer. "That's good. Now I believe you have something for me?" She held out her hand.

"Why does it matter?" Harlan asked.

"I believe we've already covered this. James? Joseph?" The two huge bodyguards at the door pulled their weapons and came forward. "If you need persuading, James and Joseph would be happy to—"

"No," said Gina, handing Adam off to Harlan before he realized what she was doing. She pulled a silver flash drive from her pocket and dropped it into the woman's outstretched palm. "Here's the study. Please, let us take Adam away from here."

"By all means." Marnie opened her arms and gestured toward the door.

"Are you really just letting us walk?" asked Harlan.

"Like you said, the bill will be law by the end of the week," said Jordan.

"And we're wanted for kidnapping and murder," said Harlan. "I guess you can let us go. We would sound pretty unhinged if we went to the authorities."

"Yes, especially if Miss Rodgers wants to keep custody of the boy. I can make all those charges go away, you know," said Marnie.

Harlan looked at Gina. Her eyes filled, and she turned to face the woman. "You can do that?"

"Why, yes, dear, of course I can. You've already lost so

much. There's no reason for you to lose your nephew and your freedom, as well."

"What would I have to do?"

"Nothing, of course. That's the beauty of it."

"And everything just goes away."

Marnie nodded. "Yes. Everything will be back the way it was."

Gina's eyes hardened.

The woman realized her mistake. "Well, no, perhaps not exactly." Marnie shook her head sadly. "I can't change everything. But I can change enough." She nodded briskly. Her heels clicked on the marble floor as she left the room.

Harlan's eyes never left Jordan's. "I hope you rot in hell." He pulled Adam closer to his chest. Gina headed for the door and Harlan followed.

"But don't you understand why, Harlan? I can do so much more this way. This one wrong seems like such a small price to pay for the good that I can do if I'm in the White House."

Harlan bowed his head. "Then you were deceived." He didn't turn around.

"What are you going to do?" Jordan asked.

"I've already done it." He turned to meet the older man's puzzled gaze. His shirt had come untucked when Gina had thrust Adam into his arms. He balanced the boy on his shoulder and raised his shirt, revealing the taped wire and microphone. "It's over."

Jordan's eyes widened, and he staggered back. "Who's listening?" The words were barely a whisper.

"You practically have your own radio show. Sandra Hall, the FBI, even Jessica Johns of Channel 8 got in on the party."

Jordan's face went ashen as he sank into the sofa. "It never occurred to me."

"That's obvious." The anger drained away and Harlan felt nothing but emptiness. Everything was gone. He looked back at Jordan. At the man he'd viewed as a father. There was nothing left. "I wish I could say I was sorry."

"But you're not."

Harlan laughed bitterly. "Hell, no. I'm just grateful Jimmy's not here to see this."

Jordan met his gaze and nodded. It was the only thing they could still agree on.

As Harlan walked to the study door with Gina beside him, the men in suits remained still at Jordan's orders.

It was his last act of kindness. There was nothing he could do. The damage was indeed done.

Laughter and music floated around them once again from the back of the house as Gina and Harlan hurried toward the front door. The bodyguards watched them cross the foyer, then closed the door to the study. Gina's hand was on the doorknob when Marnie came flying down the stairs.

"It's blank!" she screamed. "Stop them!"

What the hell?

James and Joseph burst through the study door. But they were too late.

"Run," commanded Harlan, pushing her forward and slamming the door behind them. Gina was already stumbling down the stone steps toward the car, catching herself along the way. Wind whipped dust and grit through the air as he limped hurriedly behind her. Gina opened both doors and hopped into the driver's seat.

"Gimme the keys," she demanded.

Harlan handed them over as he crawled into the backseat with Adam in his arms. "What just happened?"

"Later," she said, shoving the key in the ignition.

With a deafening crack of thunder, the heavens opened up and rain poured from the sky. James and Joseph raced down the stairs toward them.

"Hurry," he said. *What the hell had she done?*

He put Adam beside him on the floorboard and pulled the Glock from his waistband. Peering through the rain-splattered window, he searched for James and Joseph. They'd disappeared in the sudden downpour. Then he heard a shot hit metal, but he couldn't tell if the bullet was striking their Volvo or the Jag parked next to them.

He saw one of the guards taking cover behind a Bentley four cars over but unable to get a clear shot. Where the hell was the other guy? "Come on, Gina, get us out of here."

"Yeah, yeah. I'm doing it." She cranked the motor. The engine gave a rusty cough. Once, twice…then it caught and started. She threw the stick shift in reverse.

Another shot pinged off the ground where they'd been parked a moment before. That one ricocheted off the Jag.

"Duck and drive," he warned.

Five seconds later they were speeding off the estate. Two minutes later they were in heavy traffic, completely concealed and safe. Adam had slept through the entire event.

"What just happened?" Harlan asked as he buckled Adam's seatbelt and crawled into the passenger seat up front. The windshield wipers made a rhythmic swishing sound as water was swept off the glass.

"I gave Marnie a blank flash drive that I bought at the Target store on the way here tonight."

"Yeah, I figured that part out." His voice was quiet, but he felt like he had earlier today when he'd seen that dead man lying at Gina's feet. Furious and useless.

"Are you nuts?" he asked.

She flinched.

That question had come out more harshly than he'd intended. But he didn't really believe that she was losing it. Gina Rodgers could handle anything. She'd certainly proven she didn't need him.

"No," she answered, "I'm not certifiable…yet. Although there are some who might argue the point." She sighed. "I was incredibly angry. That woman had my sister murdered and a good friend killed. I couldn't stand the thought of giving her the thing that people I love the most had died for. They didn't plan to die for that study.

"And I wasn't going to give it to her. No matter what. That would have been the biggest mistake I'd ever made."

Chapter Twenty-Three

Gina watched the rain falling outside her hotel window. Would it ever stop? The weather matched her mood—or had until thirty seconds ago.

For the past three days she'd been debriefed, or whatever the FBI called it. She'd talked through the entire week with Senator Hall and various attorneys until she was blue in the face. Gina had talked to everyone about what had happened except the person she most wanted to talk to.

She stood in the center of her hotel living room suite with sweaty hands and butterflies swirling in her stomach. Harlan had called from the lobby. He was on his way up to see her.

It had been four days. Four days since they'd gone to see Jordan Bell with a wire to get Adam back. She hadn't seen Harlan since.

Senator Bell had resigned his position that night, and the next morning he'd been arrested. Marnie was nowhere to be found. The news media had been going wild with the exposé Jessica Johns was airing from the recorded tape.

Gina had given the flash drive to the Channel 8 reporter that night too. Sarah's study was going to be published. It wasn't going to be buried. Since then Gina had become a virtual prisoner in her hotel suite. But tomorrow she and Adam were leaving for Starkville.

Even though she was expecting it, the knock on the door

made her heart rate kick up a notch. She had no idea what she was going to say to Harlan.

Adam never looked up from the television. He was watching *Madagascar* for the three hundredth time via pay-per-view. Gina had given in after talking to the child psychologist Sheila had located for her.

"It's a comfort thing for him," the woman had explained. "Think of it as a soother."

Gina looked at the boy, practically comatose in front of the television and wished that Chris Rock as a talking zebra would have the same effect on her.

She took a deep breath and went to open the door. Harlan was there in jeans and a polo shirt, looking solid and wonderful, if slightly beaten up. His face was bruised and his nose was swollen.

"Hey," she said faintly, trying very hard to make eye contact but unsure of how to greet him.

Do you kiss on both cheeks someone you slept with less than a week before?

"Hey, yourself," he echoed. He kept his hands in his pockets.

"You okay?" she asked, stepping back so he could come in.

Instead, he stayed rooted to the spot, examining her with that intent gaze. She could see the dark shadows under his eyes and wondered if he'd been getting enough sleep or if that was from the beating he'd taken at Shaun's. She lost herself for a moment staring back at him.

"Hanging in there," he said, finally breaking the silence. "How about yourself?"

She took another breath. "Crazed, actually. With all the reporters, it's been bedlam here. But we're leaving tomorrow."

"I didn't realize that." He stepped just inside the entry and closed the door behind him.

"We're going to Starkville first. I've got to get Sarah's funeral arrangements made and get Adam packed up to come to Dallas. I talked to a child psychologist, and she actually recommended staying in Starkville awhile. She thought his being there would help get him stabilized before we make the move to Dallas."

"I'm glad you were able to see a doctor here."

"Yeah, we saw an autism specialist too, before the media circus began downstairs. Sandra Hall set that up. I got a crash course in autism."

"I thought you'd already had one of those." He didn't move from the doorway.

She smiled and shook her head. "Well, the goal setting and transitioning parts. She helped me figure out what Adam needs, basically how to carry on what Sarah was doing."

I won't be perfect, she thought, *but I'll be there.*

"And I hired a cleaning service to take care of Sarah's house after the break-in. They called today and said it's ready. So we're free to go."

He didn't say anything, again just stood there listening. She was babbling but couldn't seem to stop herself.

"Senator Hall has been great in terms of getting everything straightened out with the authorities. I know I have you to thank for that too. Your testimony. The man at the riverbank—he had a pretty impressive criminal record. They ruled the shooting as self-defense. The cop in Mississippi, the one Kate Brooks talked about, he has been arrested too.

"Apparently he took bribes from PharmaVax in the form of new experimental cancer drugs for his wife that aren't available yet to the public. It's really sad. He did that in exchange for what they needed done."

She took a breath. What was wrong with her? She was yammering on and on.

Stop talking. "So what about you? Why are you still here?"

Suddenly he looked shy, and she was intrigued.

"I have this for you." He reached into his back pocket and pulled out a sheet of folded paper. "I wasn't sure you'd been given a copy. It's from Sarah's flash drive at the copy shop. A letter to Adam."

Gina's hands stilled on the paper. She'd thought she had her emotions under control, but she wasn't sure she was ready for this. She glanced at Harlan. His penetrating gaze was completely focused on her. She unfolded the letter.

Dearest Adam,
The day you read this we'll both know you've grown up and I wasn't there to see it. I want to tell you how proud I am of you and how much I love you. Your aunt Gina loves you, too.

I so wanted to be there to see every new thing that you've learned and experienced. Just to be with you. I've been there in spirit.

I know you've wondered what happened and why I wasn't there. Know it was because I loved you and wanted the very best for you and I wouldn't give up until I had answers.

I'll love you always.
Mommy

Tears burned the back of Gina's throat and the edges of her eyelids, but she finished and carefully folded the letter. "Thank you for bringing this."

She looked up. "I wasn't given a copy. It will mean so much to Adam when he's old enough to…to understand." She took a deep, shuddering breath. "Surely you didn't wait four days just to give me this." She indicated the folded paper.

He didn't answer.

"When are you going home?" she asked.

"I'm not sure. I've got some military buddies around. I may hang out with them for a while. I'll probably go back to Starkville later, for a while at least."

"Oh." This wasn't going the way she'd wanted it to.

Harlan leaned against the doorframe. "So it sounds like you have a plan and everything's under control."

She laughed and thought it sounded a bit hysterical to her own ears. "Is that what you really think?"

"Well, yeah. That's what it sounds like."

She looked at him for a long time, wondered how honest to be, then decided she was a woman with absolutely nothing to lose.

"Well, I don't think you've been listening. My God, Harlan, are you blind? I'm hanging on by my fingernails, and I'm scared to death."

She got up in his face, and he backed into the doorframe. His eyes widened, but she kept going.

"I don't want to sound like I'm feeling sorry for myself, but let's catalog what's happened in the past week. I've lost my sister, my good friend, my job—which is fairly inconsequential at this point—and I killed a man. Now I'm about to start an entirely new life with my autistic nephew."

She lowered her voice. "But none of that really matters, because you've told me that I've got to do whatever it takes to get through, right? So that's what I'm doing. I've tied a knot in the end of the rope, and I'm hanging on."

"But you said you didn't need me to save you." He looked at her as if she were a somewhat skittish animal, and he was worried about setting her off again.

She vigorously nodded her head. "That's right. I don't want you to save me. But I'd like you to be with me while I deal with it all. Your presence matters, Harlan."

"But what do you want me to do?"

"You don't have to do anything. That the beauty of it. Did you read Sarah's letter?"

He nodded.

"Just being with me, being with us—me and Adam—is more than enough."

She stood close to him and pinned him with her own gaze.

"How can that be enough?" He straightened from the doorframe. "How can I be enough?" he murmured almost to himself.

She studied him. The confusion was clear in his eyes. He truly had no idea.

How could she make him understand?

Music from *Madagascar* drifted into the room. She heard the covers rustle as Adam moved around on the bed.

"Let me show you something." She walked Harlan into the bedroom where Adam was watching the movie. He was propped on his hands watching the screen, a blank expression on his face.

"Hey, buddy, look who's here."

Adam looked up from the television. A smile broke across his face. "Harlan!" he shouted and scrambled to his feet. The boy practically danced across the rug and launched himself into Harlan's arms.

Harlan stood holding Adam and staring at her with his fathomless gaze as understanding dawned. He reached for her hand, his smile matching Adam's.

"See," she whispered. "You are more than enough."

* * * * *

'I'VE FOUND HER.'

Max froze.

It was what he'd been waiting for since June, but now—now he was almost afraid to voice the question. His heart stalling, he leaned slowly back in his chair and scoured the investigator's face for clues. 'Where?' he asked, and his voice sounded rough and unused, like a rusty hinge.

'In Suffolk. She's living in a cottage.'

Living. His heart crashed back to life, and he sucked in a long, slow breath. All these months he'd feared—

'Is she well?'

'Yes, she's well.'

He had to force himself to ask the next question. 'Alone?'

The man paused. 'No. The cottage belongs to a man called John Blake. He's working away at the moment, but he comes and goes.'

God. He felt sick. So sick he hardly registered the next few words, but then gradually they sank in. 'She's got *what?*'

'Babies. Twin girls. They're eight months old.'

'Eight—?' he echoed under his breath. 'They must be his.'

He was thinking out loud, but the P.I. heard and corrected him.

'Apparently not. I gather they're hers. She's been there since mid-January last year, and they were born during the summer— June, the woman in the post office thought. She was more than helpful. I think there's been a certain amount of speculation about their relationship.'

He'd just bet there had. God, he was going to kill her. Or Blake. Maybe both of them.

'Of course, looking at the dates, she was presumably pregnant when she left you, so they could be yours, or she could have been having an affair with this Blake character before…'

He glared at the unfortunate P.I. 'Just stick to your job. I can do the math,' he snapped, swallowing the unpalatable possibility that she'd been unfaithful to him before she'd left. 'Where is she? I want the address.'

'It's all in here,' the man said, sliding a large envelope across the desk to him. 'With my invoice.'

'I'll get it seen to. Thank you.'

'If there's anything else you need, Mr Gallagher, any further information—'

'I'll be in touch.'

'The woman in the post office told me Blake was away at the moment, if that helps,' he added quietly, and opened the door.

Max stared down at the envelope, hardly daring to open it, but when the door clicked softly shut behind the P.I., he eased up the flap, tipped it and felt his breath jam in his throat as the photos spilled out over the desk.

Oh, lord, she looked gorgeous. Different, though. It took him a moment to recognise her, because she'd grown her hair, and it was tied back in a ponytail, making her look younger and somehow freer. The blond highlights were gone, and it was back to its natural soft golden-brown, with a little curl in the end of the ponytail that he wanted to thread his finger through and tug, just gently, to draw her back to him.

Crazy. She'd put on a little weight, but it suited her. She looked well and happy and beautiful, but oddly, considering how desperate he'd been for news of her for the past year—one year, three weeks and two days, to be exact—it wasn't only Julia who held his attention after the initial shock. It was the babies sitting side by side in a supermarket trolley. Two identical and absolutely beautiful little girls.

* * * * *

When Max Gallagher hires a P.I. to find his estranged wife, Julia, he discovers she's not alone—she has twin baby girls, and they might be his. Now workaholic Max has just two weeks to prove that he can be a wonderful husband and father to the family he wants to treasure.

Look for
TWO LITTLE MIRACLES
by Caroline Anderson,
available February 2009
from Harlequin Romance®

CELEBRATE
60 YEARS
OF PURE READING PLEASURE
WITH **HARLEQUIN**®!

**We'll be spotlighting a different series
every month throughout 2009
to celebrate our 60th anniversary.**

Look for Harlequin® Romance in February!

**Harlequin® Romance is celebrating by showering
you with Diamond Brides in February 2009.**

Six stories that promise to bring a touch of sparkle to
your life, with diamond proposals and dazzling weddings,
sparkling brides and gorgeous grooms!

Collect all six books in February 2009,
featuring *Two Little Miracles* by Caroline Anderson.

*Look for the Diamond Brides miniseries
in February 2009!*

HARLEQUIN® *Romance*®

This February the Harlequin® Romance series
will feature six Diamond Brides stories featuring
diamond proposals and gorgeous grooms.

Share your dream wedding proposal and you could WIN!

The most romantic entry will win a diamond
necklace and will inspire a proposal in one of
our upcoming Diamond Grooms books in 2010.

In 100 words or less, tell us the most romantic
way that you dream of being proposed to.

For more information, and to enter
the Diamond Brides Proposal contest, please visit
www.DiamondBridesProposal.com

Or mail your entry to us at:

IN THE U.S.: 3010 Walden Ave., P.O. Box 9069, Buffalo, NY 14269-9069
IN CANADA: 225 Duncan Mill Road, Don Mills, ON M3B 3K9

REQUEST YOUR FREE BOOKS!

2 FREE NOVELS
PLUS 2
FREE GIFTS!

◆ HARLEQUIN®

INTRIGUE®

Breathtaking Romantic Suspense

YES! Please send me 2 FREE Harlequin Intrigue® novels and my 2 FREE gifts (gifts are worth about $10). After receiving them, if I don't wish to receive any more books, I can return the shipping statement marked "cancel." If I don't cancel, I will receive 6 brand-new novels every month and be billed just $4.24 per book in the U.S. or $4.99 per book in Canada, plus 25¢ shipping and handling per book and applicable taxes, if any*. That's a savings of close to 15% off the cover price! I understand that accepting the 2 free books and gifts places me under no obligation to buy anything. I can always return a shipment and cancel at any time. Even if I never buy another book from Harlequin, the two free books and gifts are mine to keep forever.

182 HDN EEZ7   382 HDN EEZK

Name	(PLEASE PRINT)	
Address		Apt. #
City	State/Prov.	Zip/Postal Code

Signature (if under 18, a parent or guardian must sign)

Mail to the **Harlequin Reader Service**:
IN U.S.A.: P.O. Box 1867, Buffalo, NY 14240-1867
IN CANADA: P.O. Box 609, Fort Erie, Ontario L2A 5X3

Not valid to current subscribers of Harlequin Intrigue books.

Want to try two free books from another line?
Call 1-800-873-8635 or visit www.morefreebooks.com.

* Terms and prices subject to change without notice. N.Y. residents add applicable sales tax. Canadian residents will be charged applicable provincial taxes and GST. Offer not valid in Quebec. This offer is limited to one order per household. All orders subject to approval. Credit or debit balances in a customer's account(s) may be offset by any other outstanding balance owed by or to the customer. Please allow 4 to 6 weeks for delivery. Offer available while quantities last.

Your Privacy: Harlequin is committed to protecting your privacy. Our Privacy Policy is available online at www.eHarlequin.com or upon request from the Reader Service. From time to time we make our lists of customers available to reputable third parties who may have a product or service of interest to you. If you would prefer we not share your name and address, please check here. ☐

HI08R

You're invited to join our Tell Harlequin Reader Panel!

By joining our new reader panel you will:

- Receive Harlequin® books—they are FREE and yours to keep with no obligation to purchase anything!
- Participate in fun online surveys
- Exchange opinions and ideas with women just like you
- Have a say in our new book ideas and help us publish the best in women's fiction

In addition, you will have a chance to win great prizes and receive special gifts! See Web site for details. Some conditions apply. Space is limited.

To join, visit us at
www.TellHarlequin.com.

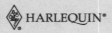
HARLEQUIN®

INTRIGUE®

COMING NEXT MONTH

#1113 UNDERCOVER STRANGER by Pat White
Assignment: The Girl Next Door
Ciara O'Malley seems as sweet and innocent as they come, but NSA agent Griffin Black knows that looks can be deceiving. He also knows that her doll museum is being used by terrorists to smuggle weapons. But when she agrees to help with the investigation, Griff wonders if this beautiful innocent he's falling for is in more danger than he realized.

#1114 PROFILE DURANGO by Carla Cassidy
Kenner County Crime Unit
FBI agent Tom Ryan had protected Calista MacBride's body, but broken her heart. Now, when strange accidents threaten Callie and Kenner County, will she be able to welcome Tom's protection yet again? Or will the pain of the past keep her from accepting that he is here to stay?

#1115 PLATINUM COWBOY by Rita Herron
Diamonds and Daddies
Flint McKade's Diamondback Ranch is being threatened, putting everything he cares about in jeopardy. Then there's the gorgeous new vet, Dr. Lora Leigh Whittaker, who seems to have her own secret agenda. But when someone tries to kill her, will she be able to open up and trust the tall, dark and handsome Flint?

#1116 EXPECTING TROUBLE by Delores Fossen
Texas Paternity: Boots and Booties
Special agent Cal Rico lives by the rules. He would never get involved with someone he has sworn to protect, which is why it comes as a shock that Texas heiress Jenna Laniere would name him as the father of her baby. With an assassin hot on Jenna's trail, though, and Cal falling hard for both mother and daughter, he faces his most important assignment yet.

#1117 CIRCUMSTANTIAL MEMORIES by Carol Ericson
Covert ops expert Ryder McClintock returns home to the shock of his life—Julia Rousseau, the woman he had loved with a burning passion, no longer remembers him. Nor does she know he's the father of her daughter...a daughter he never knew existed. But his return stirs someone else's memory, and their need for vengeance.

#1118 THE HIGH COUNTRY RANCHER by Jan Hambright
Rancher Baylor McCollough has no idea that the woman he just saved in a blizzard is Mariah Ellis, a detective sent to question him about a recent disappearance. After a harrowing past, Baylor just wants to move on with his life. When the beautiful and tenacious cop catches the eye of a killer, Baylor realizes that letting her go is impossible.

www.eHarlequin.com

HICNMBPA0109